Martin Millar was born in Scotla
is the author of such novels as *Lo...*
Wolf Girl and *The Good Fair...*
pseudonym of Martin Scott, he, as ...
a new genre: pulp fantasy noir'. *Thraxas*, the first book in his
Thraxas series, won the World Fantasy Award in 2000. As Martin
Millar and as Martin Scott, he has been widely translated.

Visit Martin Millar at:
www.martinmillar.com
www.twitter.com/MartinMillar1

Praise for Martin Millar:

'Undeniably brilliant'
Guardian

'The funniest writer in Britain today'
GQ

'Martin Millar writes like Kurt Vonnegut might have written, if
he'd been born fifty years later in a different country and hung
around with entirely the wrong sort of people'
Neil Gaiman

'Imagine Kurt Vonnegut reading Marvel Comics with The
Clash thrashing in the background. For the deceptively simple
poetry of the everyday, nobody does it better'
List

'The master of urban angst'
i-D Magazine

The Goddess of Buttercups and Daisies

MARTIN MILLAR

piatkus

PIATKUS

First published in Great Britain in 2015 by Piatkus

1 3 5 7 9 10 8 6 4 2

A CIP catalogue record for this book
is available from the British Library.

ISBN 978-0-349-40714-2

Typeset in Sabon by M Rules
Printed and bound by CPI Group (UK) Ltd, Croydon, CR0 4YY

Papers used by Piatkus are from well-managed forests
and other responsible sources.

MIX
Paper from
responsible sources
FSC® C104740

Piatkus
An imprint of
Little, Brown Book Group
100 Victoria Embankment
London EC4Y 0DY

An Hachette UK Company
www.hachette.co.uk

www.piatkus.co.uk

The City of Athens, 421 BC

Aristophanes, playwright

The agora was always busy. Everyone shopped there. Coins flew from mouth to hand, and from hand to till, as goods were bought and sold. Merchants shouted out prices, friends exchanged greetings and news, while the occasional small boy, on the run from his tutor, made a dash for the safety of the stalls. With the Dionysia festival almost due to start, it was busier than ever.

Aristophanes enjoyed his regular visits. It wasn't that he was particularly good at buying supplies, or running his household – he left most of that to his chief servant Epiktetos – but it was a fine place for observing people. Many events that ended up in his plays had their roots in the agora. People knew he was observing them. They didn't mind. Mostly it gave rise to mirth.

'Don't let Aristophanes see you doing that, he'll put you in his next comedy!'

Sosinos, at his stall selling honey cakes, greeted him warmly. 'Aristophanes, when are you going to put me on stage?'

'There's no actor handsome enough to play you, Sosinos.'

The stallholder laughed, as he always did. Sosinos had a reasonable stock of cakes on display, which wasn't always the case. After ten years of war, with no end in sight, supplies of everything had run low. Sosinos's honey cakes were one of the few treats left in the city.

'Haven't seen you for a few days. Busy at rehearsals?'

Aristophanes nodded.

'How's it going?'

Aristophanes made a face, and asked Sosinos if he still gambled.

'All the time.'

'Then bet on the opposition. My play's a disaster.'

'Come on, Aristophanes, it can't be that bad.'

'It is. There's more chance of the Goddess Athena turning up here with a supply of honey cakes than there is of me winning first prize this year.'

Bremusa, Amazon

Bremusa hung back while the Goddess Athena spoke to the Goddess Hera. Bremusa had been on Mount Olympus for almost eight hundred years, but she'd never really felt that Hera accepted her. Perhaps because she was an Amazon. Or perhaps Hera just didn't like latecomers. There were many people whom Hera didn't like.

'I hear you've been talking to Helios.' Hera's voice carried the faint tone of disapproval that residents of Olympus were used to hearing.

Athena smiled pleasantly. She was never intimidated by Hera. 'Indeed. I asked him to provide fine weather for the Dionysia.'

'Really? I never much cared for that festival. But then, I never much cared for Athens.'

That was something of an insult, Athena being patron of Athens.

'But perhaps they deserve a good festival,' continued Hera. 'The way things are going, it might be their last.'

She smiled and went on her way, up the mountain. Athena looked momentarily troubled. Hera's barb had landed. The goddess knew that the war between Athens and Sparta was costing her city dearly. The Athenians may have had the finest navy but the Spartan army dominated the field. In the campaigning season, the Athenians were forced to withdraw behind their city walls, while the Spartans destroyed their crops and their lands. The city could not sustain that indefinitely.

'Sparta isn't doing that well either,' muttered Athena, which was true. Ten years of warfare had almost brought both city-states to their knees.

Bremusa followed Athena into the goddess's mansion. When Bremusa had first seen the building, shortly after Athena plucked her off the battlefield at Troy, she'd been startled by its luxury. The marble columns, the pool, the Corinthian couches, the statues, the amphoras – all had been new to her, and startling to a woman raised among the frugal Amazons. She was used to it now.

'It's time the war ended,' said Athena.

'Aren't they holding a peace conference?'

Athena frowned. 'It's not going as well as I'd hoped. When both of their war leaders were killed, I thought they'd make some progress.'

'Athens and Sparta have never had any problem finding new war leaders. Why not just let them fight it out?'

The Goddess Athena was blond-haired and grey-eyed. That had been another surprise to Bremusa, the first time she'd encountered her.

'The war's gone on long enough, Bremusa. I love Athens but I'm also patron of Sparta. I don't want to see any more destruction. They need time to recover.'

'Maybe they're weak and deserve to be destroyed.'

Athena smiled. 'Show some sympathy.'

'I never gave up a fight.'

'You'd have died at Troy if I hadn't snatched you away before Idomeneus's spear pierced your heart.'

'I wasn't complaining,' said Bremusa, rather tersely. She didn't like to be reminded of her defeat at the hands of Idomeneus of Crete.

'I know. When I brought you to Mount Olympus you wanted to go back and fight again. But you're an Amazon, Bremusa. Not everyone has your endless enthusiasm for war. Look at all these prayers from Greeks, asking for peace.'

Athena indicated the great cedar-wood table in front of the

shrine, on which, every day, her servants carefully laid out the prayers made by Athenians to the goddess. Each one was carefully transcribed onto a neat piece of parchment. There was one very large bundle; prayers asking for peace.

Bremusa pointed to a smaller pile beside them. 'What about those?'

'Prayers for victory,' said the goddess. 'Not so many.'

'Still a reasonable bundle though. Not everyone in Athens wants peace.'

'The weapon-makers are a powerful lobby. They've got some ambitious generals on their side.'

Bremusa noticed another pile of prayers at the corner of the table. 'What are they?'

The goddess sighed. 'Prayers from Luxos.' She picked up one of the pieces of parchment. '"Dear Goddess Athena. Please help me become a successful lyric poet. No one will give me a chance because I'm the son of a poor oarsman. I know I can succeed as a poet if I can only get started. You have always been my favourite goddess. Love, Luxos."'

Bremusa, rather grim-faced as a rule, couldn't prevent herself from smiling. 'He doesn't give up, does he? How many's that?'

'Nine this week.'

'Does he perform the appropriate sacrifices when he prays?'

'No. But he did leave a daisy on my altar.' The goddess stared at the tiny flower. 'It's not the greatest offering I've ever had.'

Polykarpos, Tavern Owner

The Trident had once been the busiest and merriest tavern south of the acropolis. While the wealthy citizens of Athens entertained themselves at their symposiums, the poorer citizens went to Polykarpos's. It was cheerful, noisy and profitable. Polykarpos was an excellent landlord and he'd made the Trident into a welcoming retreat for friends, acquaintances, travellers, prostitutes, singers, dancers, drinkers and anyone else who needed a cup or two of wine after a hard day's work. Athens was a hard-working city. The citizens believed in it. They strove to improve it. They were entitled to their leisure.

Decline had set in some years ago. As the war dragged on, and the city suffered, so did the tavern. For the first few years, citizens had maintained their optimism. People might grumble as they were called up into the army, but they put on their hoplite armour, picked up their shields, and went away to serve loyally, believing in the promises of the politicians and orators. For a while, these promises came true. Athens already ruled a large maritime empire and at first it seemed they were going to get the better of the Spartans. Then came the reverses. The war started to go badly. The Spartans marched over from the Peloponnese and began destroying Athenian lands. Athenian colonies took the opportunity to revolt and stopped paying taxes. The city's income began to shrink. The Trident was no longer such a happy place.

Each year the situation had become worse. After ten years of fighting, Polykarpos was fortunate to serve a few customers a day. Those who did arrive barely had the money for a small cup of wine. Even if they had, the Trident often had little to sell them. Like everything else, wine was in short supply. Athenian vineyards had been destroyed, and there was precious little coming in through the port at Piraeus.

The elderly citizen Methodios appeared through the front door. Polykarpos hadn't seen him for a while, though he used to be a regular. He mended fishing nets down at the harbour. He took out a small silver coin and asked for a jug of wine.

'Business picking up?'

Methodios scowled. 'What business? I've got no workers left. Every young man in Piraeus is rowing a warship. Even the slaves were freed so they could be recruited. There's no one left to mend

7

fishing nets. The only reason I've got a coin to my name is because I was called up for jury duty.'

A young prostitute, momentarily hopeful at the appearance of a customer, looked away, disappointed.

Methodios sighed as he sipped his wine. 'I fought the Persians. Desperate times, but they weren't as bad as this. How long can it go on for?'

The landlord didn't reply. Athenians had been asking that for years, and no one had an answer.

'Some Spring Festival this is going to be,' muttered the old net-mender.

'Maybe something will come of the peace conference.'

'Not likely, from what I hear.'

Polykarpos had noticed a change in attitude among his customers recently. All of them had been involved in the war in some way or another. A few years ago, there had been no talk of peace. That might have been seen as bowing down to the Spartans, which they would never do. Now, people weren't so sure. Even when news came in of the powerful Athenian navy destroying Spartan settlements, it wasn't greeted with the same enthusiasm it once had been. The Spartans, after all, were busy destroying theirs.

'It might help if our own politicians could agree among themselves,' said Polykarpos.

Methodios snorted as he sipped his wine. 'Damned politicians. Only interested in lining their own pockets. I hate them.'

Luxos the Poet

Luxos rose, poked his head out the window, and smiled.

'It's a beautiful morning. Good day for writing poetry.'

He busied himself with breakfast, which didn't take long as the only food available in his tiny dwelling was a small scrap of stale bread, hardly enough for a child's snack. Luxos, however, was used to going without food. In the poor part of the city, many people were hungry these days. Luxos's poverty was more extreme than most, but he had an optimistic nature and was sure something would turn up. He was nineteen, orphaned, and apparently without prospects, but he had belief in his own abilities, and a great faith in the Goddess Athena.

He addressed his stale piece of bread, quoting a few lines from Archilochus:

> *If he keeps complaining of woeful misfortunes,*
> *No citizen will take pleasure in feasting,*
> *It's true my noble soul has suffered in the roaring sea*
> *And my heart has been broken*
> *But to woes incurable,*
> *The gods have ordained the remedy of staunch endurance.*
> *So banish your grief,*
> *Endure, and prosper.*

Luxos washed down the stale bread with his last remaining mouthful of cheap wine.

I can really feel things turning my way. I'm sure Athena is going to help me any day now.

He put on his worn sandals and his ragged chiton and set off into the sunshine to see what he could find.

General Lamachus

General Lamachus met with General Acanthus far outside the city walls, away from prying eyes. With the Spartan delegation already in Athens for the peace conference, it wasn't so strange for an Athenian general to be talking with a Spartan, but their business was private. Acanthus sat erect on his horse, his red cloak and long hair easily identifying him as a Spartan. Lamachus's cloak was blue and his hair was short, but the Athenian cavalryman didn't feel they were really so different.

'What's the mood among the Spartan delegation?'

'Still undecided. But I suspect they're leaning towards voting for peace, and signing the treaty. What about Athens?'

'The same.'

There was a pause. They looked back towards the walls. The spring sun was overhead, already hot.

'I don't want that to happen,' said the Spartan general.

'Nor do I.'

'It won't take too much for me to persuade the Spartans not to sign.' Acanthus looked pointedly at Lamachus.

'I don't control the Athenian delegation,' Lamachus told him. 'There has to be a vote in the assembly. A lot of people want peace.'

The Spartan sneered. 'Athens pays too much attention to the people.'

'I know. But there are ways of influencing them.'

Aristophanes

Aristophanes could still remember the pride he'd felt when he first walked up the Pnyx to take his seat with the rest of the citizens in the Athenian assembly. He was eighteen, and old enough to vote on public matters. It was a proud moment. A decade or so later, his enthusiasm had dimmed. Allowing every adult male citizen to discuss and vote on every decision was excellent in theory, but it hadn't rescued them from ten years of war.

Even though his plays had made him a well-known figure in Athens, Aristophanes wouldn't have claimed to have much influence in the assembly. You needed a very loud voice to sway the crowd.

A loud voice, and a lack of scruples, thought the playwright sourly, as he watched Hyperbolus haranguing the assembly. Hyperbolus, a lamp-maker by trade, was the extreme democrats' new hero. Aristophanes loathed him.

'Nicias and his peace-loving friends are traitors!' roared Hyperbolus, shaking his fist. 'Anyone wanting to make peace with the Spartans is a coward! The rich people of Athens would rather cosy up with the Spartans than give the poor people of Athens their fair share of the wealth.'

Many citizens shouted their approval. Nicias, elderly now, sat with a dignified look on his face.

As Hyperbolus carried on, Aristophanes nudged Hermogenes, who sat beside him in the open-air assembly.

'Is this oaf ever going to stop speaking? We've got work to do.'

'I don't see us getting to rehearsals any time soon,' whispered Hermogenes. 'Nicias is going to make a reply.'

Aristophanes groaned. 'The dignified but stumbling oratory of Nicias. We'll be here all day.'

'He's not such a bad orator,' said Hermogenes. 'Not many laughs, but he makes his point.'

'Eventually, I suppose.'

Aristophanes yawned. With the sun blazing down, and the effects of last night's wine still not fully out of his system, he was finding the assembly more than usually irksome.

'It's not like we're going to come to any sort of decision today anyway.'

Hermogenes nodded. There was no clear majority either way, and neither the speeches of Hyperbolus nor Nicias would dramatically change things. Eventually the assembly came to an end without taking a vote, and the citizens trooped back down the hill, dissatisfied. Aristophanes and Hermogenes headed towards their rehearsal space.

'I hate Hyperbolus.' Aristophanes sounded bitter. 'I'd write another scene attacking him if it didn't make me feel cheap even mentioning him. Kleon was despicable, but at least he was coherent. Vaguely intelligent too. Hyperbolus is just a loud-mouthed thug.'

Hermogenes shrugged. Aristophanes looked at him suspiciously. 'Did you just shrug?'

'Maybe.'

'Why?'

'No reason.'

They walked on. Aristophanes felt a nagging unease. 'I really don't see why you shrugged. Did you just shrug again? What's with all the shrugging?'

'Nothing.'

'There must be something. No one keeps shrugging for no reason.'

'Maybe I don't view Hyperbolus quite as badly as you.'

Aristophanes came to an abrupt halt. 'What?'

'Maybe I don't think he's all bad. All right, he is a loudmouth. Probably a thug, too. That doesn't mean everything he says is wrong.'

Aristophanes was aghast. 'I can't believe I'm hearing this. You mean you support him?'

'Not exactly. I just don't think he's as bad as you make out. So he accuses some of the wealthy citizens of being Spartan sympathisers. That's not that hard to believe, is it? It's not like they've got the best interests of the common oarsman at heart, is it?'

'I've never heard such nonsense!' cried Aristophanes. 'These people aren't trying to prolong the war because they've got the best interest of the common citizen at heart! They're just after profit and glory.'

'Some of them, perhaps. But the democrats were the ones who got decent pay for the oarsmen, and my father was in the navy.'

'What use is decent pay if everyone's farm is destroyed, and all the young men die in battle?'

Aristophanes and his assistant glared at each other for a few seconds. They'd worked together for several years. Normally, it was a good working relationship.

'We should get to rehearsals,' said Aristophanes.

They walked on. Aristophanes fumed briefly over the argument, but quickly forgot about it while considering the problems he'd been having in rehearsals. His new play was called *Peace*. Aristophanes was keen for it to entertain the audience at the festival, and even keener for it to win first prize.

It didn't take long for things to go wrong. Aristophanes was telling his lead actor, Philippus, that he'd rewritten the opening speech – largely due to Philippus's inability to deliver the original properly – when his assistant Hermogenes bustled up, looking worried.

'Aristophanes! There's a problem with our penises!'

'What?'

'They're too floppy!'

Aristophanes took a step backwards. So did Philippus.

'Speak for yourself,' said Aristophanes.

'I've never had any problem,' said Philippus.

'I mean our onstage phalluses! Look!'

He pointed to the small rehearsal stage, where the chorus was assembling, some already wearing their masks, some still carrying them. Each was wearing a simple rehearsal robe but they all had on the standard comedy phallus, an obligatory accessory for the Athenian comic chorus. Some hung down about twelve inches, others eighteen.

'What's wrong?'

'The big ones won't erect properly!'

Aristophanes hurried over to the chorus. They already had problems with just about every aspect of the production. The last thing they needed was a phallus malfunction.

'Let me see.'

The actors in the chorus pulled the internal drawstrings that made their penises go erect. It was a classic move in comedy. All playwrights used it. A good Athenian comedy needed huge penises going up and down at regular intervals.

Aristophanes frowned. The twelve-inch phalluses were standing up fairly well, but the eighteen-inch models were drooping hopelessly. It made for a sorry sight. There were times when a droopy phallus was the right thing for your comedy, but they had to be able to stand up when required. Everyone knew that.

'What's the matter?' Aristophanes was irate. 'Who made these?'

'Normal prop workshop. But they say they can't get the correct materials. The war . . .'

Aristophanes clenched his fist. 'Damn these Spartans. And damn these politicians who won't make peace. Now they're ruining my chorus's phalluses.'

'Well,' said Philippus, 'the smaller ones're not too bad, they're standing up all right.'

Aristophanes waved this away. The smaller penis was only twelve inches long.

'I can't send my chorus out with only twelve inches dangling in front of them. The audience will jeer them off the stage. I'd be ridiculed. Did you see the size of Eupolis's last year? When his chorus turned round they almost decapitated the front row. Look, Hermogenes, these just won't do. Tell Leon in the prop department we need them bigger and better. And harder.'

'We don't have any money for materials. The props department is already scavenging around for scraps.'

Aristophanes could feel his fists clenching tighter. His production had been starved of money from the outset, thanks to the Dionysian drama committee giving him the producer from Hades.

'Dammit! A soon as Antimachus was assigned to us, I knew there'd be trouble. He hates me. Eupolis gets Simonides as his producer, and Simonides is rich. My rivals are awash with money and I'm struggling with inferior phalluses!'

By now he was shaking with anger. 'If I don't win first prize for comedy this year there's going to be trouble. Tell our so-called – our prop designer—'

Aristophanes was interrupted by a tug on his tunic. As he turned round his face fell.

'Luxos? Who let you in here?'

'Hello, Aristophanes. Would you like to hear my new poem?'

Aristophanes sighed. Luxos was nineteen, the son of an oarsman. He wanted to be a poet. Zeus only knew why.

'I don't have time right now, Luxos.'

'But it's my new poem about the Battle of Salamis!'

'What would you know about Salamis?'

'My grandfather fought there.'

'Did you consider following him into the navy?'

Luxos looked a little downcast. He was a pretty young boy, but he wasn't athletic.

'They said I was too weak to pull an oar. Won't you listen to my poem?'

'I'm too busy.'

'But I want to be a lyric poet.'

'Where's your lyre?'

Luxos looked embarrassed. 'It's ... being repaired.'

Aristophanes glared at Luxos. It wasn't the first time the putative young poet had interrupted his work. Aristophanes would have thrown him out of the theatre if they hadn't both been members of the Pandionis tribe. That did bring certain obligations. You were meant to be civil to fellow members, and help them out if possible. However, while Aristophanes did occasionally farm out some lyric writing to his staff, neither he nor anyone else was ever going to trust Luxos to write poetry for them, with his effeminately long, tousled hair, his obvious poverty, and his lack of training. He was wasting his time.

15

Luxos sensed his thoughts. 'No one will give me a chance. Just because I'm the son of an oarsman ...'

'Face it, Luxos, few great Athenian writers have come from families of rowers. You weren't even educated.'

'I educated myself! How about giving me the poetry spot before your play starts?'

Before the comedies were presented at the festival, it was customary for one of Athens' great lyric poets to entertain the crowd with a few well-chosen pieces, to get them in the mood. As with everything connected with the festival, it was an honour to be selected.

'Luxos, before my actors walk onstage, the crowd will be entertained by one of Athens' great poets. Does that include you?'

'Yes!'

'Only in your own mind.'

'But I could do it if I got the chance.'

'Come back in a few years when you've made your reputation and I'll consider it.'

'It's not fair,' said Luxos.

'We've been at war for ten years. Nothing's fair any more.'

Aristophanes turned away. Behind him, Luxos had started reciting, but he wasn't listening.

Shout to him! We shall sing of Dionysus on these holy days: he has been absent for twelve months, but now the springtime is here, and all the flowers.

General Lamachus

General Lamachus didn't enjoy being involved with politics in Athens. It had always been troublesome; since the franchise had been extended to almost every man in the city, he'd found it intolerable. He said as much to Euphranor, when they met in the Pegasus barber shop.

'We have a chaotic, ineffective government that can barely make a decision. When they do, it's liable to be wrong. Do these people think they're free? As far as I can see they follow the herd. Whoever shouts the loudest, and promises the most reward for the least effort, gets their votes.'

The general warmed to his theme. 'I hate the Spartans but I envy them too. They have two kings, and some ephors, and they make all the decisions. None of this consulting the entire population, with the endless slanging matches we have in our assembly. Every petty demagogue saying whatever suits him best, never mind what the city needs. I hate to be involved with these people.'

Euphranor nodded. He'd been a strong warrior in his time. Now he was grey-haired and overweight, and he wore a chiton a little too fancy for a man of his age. Nonetheless, he was still a powerful character. His weapons factory had made him one of the richest men in Athens. 'It's unfortunate, but we need to be involved. We can't let the peace conference succeed.'

The general scowled. 'It's demeaning for men like us to be associated with a loud-mouthed rabble-rouser like Hyperbolus.'

'I know. But there's no one like him for stirring up the crowd.'

Their conversation paused as the barber and his slave attended to Euphranor's beard. Lamachus wondered what General Acanthus and his Spartan delegation were doing at this moment. Not sitting in a barber's, that was certain. *Long-haired Spartans.* He was sure he could lead Athens to victory over them, if only he was given the chance.

'So what's the feeling in the rest of the city?'

'Still mixed,' said Euphranor. 'I've given Hyperbolus and his party plenty of silver to spread around, but even so there are a lot of people pushing for peace.' He paused, and looked momentarily awkward. 'I paid a visit to Kleonike.'

'Her again?' General Lamachus was exasperated. 'We don't need help from some renegade priestess.'

'No harm in covering all the angles. Kleonike is a clever woman. And fond of money, as it happens.'

Kleonike, Priestess

The silver mines at Laurium had brought a lot of wealth to Athens. Themistocles used the money to pay for two hundred triremes, setting them on the road to power. Athenian coins were used all over the civilised world. It was highest quality silver. The priestess Kleonike regretted that she'd never seen any great share of it. As a loyal Athenian priestess of thirty years' standing, she thought she might have been better remunerated. When Euphranor, who had more than his share of Athenian silver, visited the temple with some specific requests, backed up by some solid currency, she didn't mind accommodating him.

Euphranor was a fool, of course. No one but a fool would ask an Athenian priestess to summon Laet.

She knelt in front of the altar. Egyptian incense swirled around her head. 'Come to Athens, Laet, bringer of discord. Come to Athens, and let the strife continue.'

Bremusa, Amazon Warrior

Bremusa had noticed they didn't have that many emergencies on Mount Olympus. Fewer than they used to anyway. There didn't seem to be so many semi-divine adventurers in Greece these days, causing problems. However, from the Goddess Athena's expression as she flew out of the private shrine in her mansion, she knew something bad had happened.

'Bremusa, I just received terrible news from Delphi! Some corrupt priestess in Athens has summoned Laet!'

'Who's Laet?'

Athena gave her a rather angry glance. 'How can you not know who Laet is?'

'You have so many of these semi-divine figures. I lose track.'

'You have been here for more than seven hundred years,' said the goddess. 'I thought you'd know them all by now. Laet is the granddaughter of Eris, goddess of strife, discord and war. You remember the trouble she caused with that golden apple. And if that's not bad enough, Laet is also the daughter of Ate, the spirit of delusion, infatuation and reckless folly.'

'Some parentage. Who's her father?'

'No one knows. But if he was unwise enough to fall for Ate, I doubt he's still around.'

'So what's this Laet like?'

The goddess made a face. 'With Strife as a grandmother and Reckless Folly as a mother? Laet is the very embodiment of utter foolishness. She's the spirit of choosing the worst option on every occasion. She has a baleful influence on all who encounter her. Which means ...'

'She's not the kind of person you'd want at a peace conference?'

'Exactly.' The Goddess Athena looked troubled. 'If she enters Athens unchecked, there will be chaos. The peace conference will fall apart.'

Somehow Bremusa couldn't see this as such a great crisis. 'They've been fighting for ten years anyway.'

'Bremusa, I want peace! My cities need respite.'

'You've participated in a lot of war in your time ... Athena Promachos, leader in battle.'

'Well now I'm acting as Athena Polias, protector of the city. And I want peace.'

The goddess drummed her fingertips on a gilded table, causing the golden bowls of grapes to vibrate.

'I'd stop Laet myself if Zeus didn't prevent Olympians entering the cities during festivals. There's nothing else for it, Bremusa – you'll have to stop her for me.'

That was a suggestion the Amazon liked. She drew her sword. 'I'll make short work of her.'

'Put your sword away. Laet can't die in Athens. Her malevolent spirit would curse the city. I need you to stop her tactfully.'

Bremusa didn't like that so much. 'Tactfully? How?'

'Outwit her.'

'That's never been my strongest point.'

'I have faith in you,' said Athena.

'Can't I just chop her head off? I'm good at that.'

The goddess pursed her lips. 'I'll find someone to help you with the outwitting.'

Luxos

Luxos hadn't really expected that Aristophanes would let him write lyrics for his plays, though he did hold out some hope that he might allow him the valuable position of reciting to the audience before the plays were staged. While Aristophanes had dismissed the suggestion out of hand, Luxos didn't give up hope. He had a naturally optimistic spirit. Besides, he had other avenues to explore, and wasn't finished with Aristophanes yet.

'I hear you're going to a drinking party at Callias's house.'

'We call them symposiums. What of it?'

'It will be full of literary people. Take me with you.'

Aristophanes seemed surprised. 'Why would I do that?'

'Why not? Callias is the richest man in Athens. It will be full of influential people. You could invite me to recite my poetry.'

'The evenings are meant to be enjoyable.'

'My poetry is enjoyable! I'm sweeping away the old conventions! If these smart people heard me they'd be impressed, I know it.'

Aristophanes sighed. He did that a lot when he was talking to Luxos. 'And give you a spot at the festival, I suppose?'

'Yes!'

'Luxos, we've been over this already. The Dionysia festival is for established names only. They don't have a beginner's section.'

'I'm not a beginner! I've been writing and singing and playing for years!'

'Busking at the harbour doesn't count. Athens invites all the best poets from all over Greece, Luxos. They're not going to let you on the same stage as them. I'm not giving you the lyric poetry spot before my play, it's for established names only.'

'How will I ever get established if no one will give me a chance?'

Aristophanes looked momentarily sympathetic, but behind him his assistant was talking loudly to someone, distracting him.

'Really, Luxos, I don't have time for this. If you're so keen to perform at the theatre, shouldn't you be talking to the festival curators? They decide who's allowed to enter.'

'I tried. They won't talk to me. Nor will the paredroi.'

There were ten curators taking charge of the festival. Above them were two important officials, the paredroi. Luxos had attempted to see them all. Most times he didn't make it past their assistants, and when he did, he was met with indifference and annoyance.

'How come Athens is meant to be so democratic about everything, but when it comes to poetry you don't have a chance unless you're rich? It's not fair. Let me come to the symposium.'

'No. It's invitation only. For superior artistic intellects.'

'And flute girls.' The symposiums held by the upper classes tended not to be entirely intellectual affairs.

'A few flute girls may be in attendance,' admitted Aristophanes.

When Hermogenes rushed up with a report, the playwright turned to him with the sort of urgency commonly seen on the battlefield when a messenger arrived with news of enemy positions.

'The prop-maker says he can get them up to fourteen inches. Any longer, they'll go floppy.'

Aristophanes threw up his hands in frustration. 'Fourteen inches? That's nowhere near long enough! What's the point of me writing the funniest dialogue if Eupolis has bigger penises? You know what the Athenian audience is like. They're all morons.'

'Even Socrates?'

'He's the worst of the lot. As for Euripides ... '

Hermogenes looked thoughtful. 'Perhaps we're worrying unnecessarily. Everyone in Athens is short of materials. Eupolis and Leucon's choruses might not have such big stage-penises either.'

'That's possible.' Aristophanes frowned. He looked a little older than his years. When some of the people he'd attacked in his plays hadn't taken it well, and prosecuted him in court, it had aged him.

'Luxos, when did you last eat properly?'

The young poet was surprised at the question. He was always hungry, but he'd grown used to it.

'Eh ... I can't remember ... '

'Do you want to earn some money?'

'Yes!'

'Then listen. I have a mission for you.'

Idomeneus of Crete

Idomeneus of Crete never thought he'd end up as nursemaid to a semi-divine figure like Laet. There again, he never thought he'd live for eight hundred years. 'Nursemaid' wasn't quite accurate. It wasn't as if Laet didn't have a lot of power. She had, but she wasn't very practical. She didn't know how to rent a room, or book passage at sea, or light a campfire, or anything like that.

Sitting in the Trident tavern, waiting for her to arrive, Idomeneus was listening to the conversations going on around him. It was a habit he'd picked up from his time with Laet. It amused him, because he knew what was going to happen if she decided to exert her powers. Everyone in the vicinity would do precisely the wrong thing. Anyone making a decision would make the wrong choice. He'd seen it happen hundreds of times, and it still amused him. At the next table, for instance, a solid-looking citizen was trying to persuade another, rather shabbier, citizen, to invest money in a merchant voyage to Libya. Though he was describing the potential profits in glowing terms, the shabby citizen was having none of it.

'A trading voyage to Libya? With enemy warships every-where? Forget it, it's too risky.'

'The Athenian navy will protect my ship.'

'The Athenian navy will be busy ravaging Spartan lands. Your ship will go down to pirates, if it doesn't sink in a storm.'

Idomeneus knew that the shabby citizen spoke wisely. A merchant voyage to Libya was a risk.

'You'd better get out of here before she arrives,' he muttered to himself.

The tavern was quiet, far quieter than Idomeneus had expected.

'It must be true what people are saying,' he mused. Athens is on its knees. Only a severe shortage of money could keep these degenerate Athenians out of their taverns.

The landlord had a hangdog expression, the sort a man wore when business was bad, with no prospect of things improving. When Idomeneus noticed his expression change abruptly to one of puzzlement and wonder, he knew Laet had arrived. She generally affected people like that. Laet was the sort of exotic beauty you didn't see every day. The contrast between the paleness of her skin and the deep black of her hair and eyes was startling. Her features were perfect. Not only that, she projected the sort of aura that could render a man speechless. She wasn't the sort of woman low-lives called out after in the street. When she swept by, they went quiet.

Idomeneus rose to greet her. Laet looked around at the plain tavern walls and the bare floorboards. 'Is this the best you could find?'

'It's all we can afford till we get paid.'

Laet shrugged her shoulders, quite elegantly. She felt it was better for her image to be seen in wealthier surroundings, but she didn't really care. She'd slept rough in the country plenty of times. Laet was tougher than she looked.

Conversation started up again at the next table.

'Now I think about it, a voyage to Libya does sound like a good business opportunity. I'd be silly not to invest. I'll go and dig up my savings from the garden.'

Idomeneus smiled. *Poor shabby citizen. He should have left before Laet arrived.*

The spirit of bad decisions had arrived in Athens. That did not bode well for anyone.

Aristophanes

In desperation, Aristophanes hunted down his producer Antimachus. He knew he'd find him at the Lyceum gymnasium,

24

where he was friends with Gelus, one of the gymnastae responsible for training the athletes. It meant a long walk, and he couldn't really spare the time, but his play was now so short of funds that something had to be done.

The Lyceum was east of the city walls, north of the River Ilissus. As Aristophanes approached he caught sight of a group of naked teenage boys practising their discus-throwing, just beyond the grove of olive trees that marked the outskirts of the Lyceum. It struck him that he hadn't been here in over a year, though he used to visit often; exercising, meeting with friends, listening to the occasional philosopher discourse. The three gymnasia outside the walls were popular meeting places, but with writing and rehearsals he just hadn't had the time. As Aristophanes passed the lithe, athletic, naked youths, he suddenly felt much older than a man of thirty should. He used to be active like them, but now ... He sighed and shook his head. Being a playwright in Athens was a stressful business. When Kleon had prosecuted him, his health had suffered. At least Kleon was gone now. Killed in battle. Best thing the Spartans ever did, in Aristophanes' opinion.

He found Antimachus sitting in the shade of an olive tree, watching his friend Gelus teach wrestling moves to a group of eighteen-year-olds. The young wrestlers, also naked, looked even more athletic than the discus-throwers. Again Aristophanes felt out of condition. That wasn't something Antimachus worried about; he was one of Athens' larger citizens. He saw Aristophanes coming and didn't bother to pretend to be pleased.

Aristophanes knew there was no point in making a tactful approach. 'Antimachus, I've got no scenery, no props and I can't afford to hire a decent choreographer. You have to give me more funds.'

Antimachus shrugged. Though he was sitting in the shade, he was sweating as profusely as the athletes. He dabbed his face with a fancy piece of cloth.

'I can't do that.'

'My rivals both have bigger budgets! Eupolis and Leucon are recruiting all the best talent!'

'Maybe they're just better playwrights than you?'

Aristophanes glared at him, and once again cursed the day he'd been assigned as his producer. It was all meant to be done randomly, by drawing lots, but he had his suspicions.

'Antimachus, ever since you were selected as my choregos, you've put obstacles in my way. I don't understand why. Wealthy citizens are usually proud to produce a comedy. The post of choregos is meant to be an honour.'

'Then I'm honoured,' said Antimachus. 'But you can't have any more money. I can't afford it.'

'You were pleased enough to put on your best clothes and take part in the opening procession! You didn't mind the applause then, did you?'

'I was simply doing my duty after being selected,' said Antimachus. 'That doesn't mean I can provide you with endless funds.'

'Is this all because I once mildly criticised you in a play?'

Antimachus growled. The languid expression he'd been attempting to maintain vanished. 'Mildly criticised? You ridiculed me in the vilest of terms. Your actors pointed at me from the stage and threatened to throw dung at me! I was a laughing stock. Too bad for you I ended up as your producer this year.'

There was a cry from one of the wrestlers as he was thrown heavily to the ground, followed by a sharp reprimand from Gelus the gymnastis, telling him to get up and stop complaining.

'If my play looks cheap on stage it will reflect badly on you.'

'Really?' A cunning look spread over Antimachus's florid features. 'I think a lot of people might be pleased that I didn't support your play. It's called *Peace*, isn't it?'

'Yes. What of it?'

'There are important citizens in Athens who won't look kindly on a playwright asking the city to make peace.'

'Important citizens? Like your friend Euphranor with his weapons factory?'

'Him, and plenty of others. You should stay out of politics, Aristophanes. If you get too involved, you never know what harm you might come to.'

Aristophanes left the Lyceum seething with the injustice of it all. He scowled at the discus-throwers on his way out. Citizens generally appreciated the strength and beauty of the naked, oiled athletes, but by now he was finding them depressing. He managed a respectful nod towards the shrine of the Muses as he left, but other than that he walked home depressed, completely absorbed by thoughts of failure.

Bremusa

Bremusa and the Goddess Athena walked unseen down the slopes of Mount Olympus. It was some time since Bremusa had left Olympus on a mission. It felt good to be back in her leather armour. Athena had expressed some doubts about her wearing armour to Athens, fearing it would make her conspicuous, but on consideration she gave her consent.

'You're going to look conspicuous whatever you wear, but the city will be full of visitors for the Dionysia, so it shouldn't matter that much. Try not to draw your sword, the Athenians won't like any trouble at their festival.'

'Will there be other warriors in the city?'

'All the Athenians are warriors, in a way.'

'You mean they're shopkeepers who pick up a spear when they have to.'

'Don't disparage them. They've fought valiantly when it was

27

necessary. If it wasn't for Athens, Greece would be a Persian colony by now. But there won't be anyone looking for a fight at the moment, I shouldn't think. Everyone will be too busy enjoying the festival.'

'What's the Dionysia like?'

The goddess looked surprised. 'Haven't you ever been?'

Bremusa shook her head.

'Bremusa, you've been with me on Mount Olympus for more than seven hundred years. How can it be that you've never taken a trip to the great Dionysia?'

'I suppose I never had any reason.'

Athena smiled. 'The Spring Festival in Athens is marvellous. Tragedies, comedies, music, song, dancing – you'll like it.'

'No I won't.'

'I'm sure you will.'

'I really think I won't.'

'Didn't Amazons ever have any fun?'

'We liked killing people.'

They walked on downhill in silence, passing through the region where only the divines could go, and out into the world of mortal men. It was sunny and pleasant, more pleasant than Bremusa had expected.

'I still don't see why we need to recruit some river goddess,' she said.

'Metricia's not a goddess, she's just a river spirit. I told you Zeus will no longer allow gods or goddesses to enter Athens for the Dionysia. But Metricia will be a useful companion for you. She has a lot of power. She'll locate Laet, and I expect her capacity for spiritual healing will dispel her bad energy.'

Bremusa nodded. She wasn't that keen on travelling with a companion she'd never met, but she supposed it made sense. Once they reached Athens, they'd need to find Laet quickly, before she did too much damage.

The aura of the Divine Mount Olympus stretched out for

some way beyond its confines. They passed a centaur as they entered the woods, and Bremusa thought she heard some giggling in the undergrowth, from nymphs perhaps.

'The temple isn't far,' said the goddess.

They passed over a small hillock, entered another wooded grove, then halted in surprise. There in front of them was the temple and shrine of the river spirit Metricia, but it was in ruins. Slates had fallen from the roof and the walls were crumbling. Vines grew around the marble pillars. Athena frowned, quite deeply. She walked towards the entrance but Bremusa quickly stepped in front of her. She intended to go in first, in case there was anything dangerous inside.

The temple had only two rooms, and the wall between them was damaged. Bremusa thought it was unoccupied till she saw a young woman asleep on a couch. She had a blanket draped half on, half off, and her long, black, wavy hair was splayed over the cushion she used as a pillow. Beside the couch were several empty amphoras of wine. The sight of a young woman, apparently inebriated in a holy shrine, irritated her.

'On your feet for the Goddess Athena!' she cried.

The young woman opened her eyes. She looked at them, without rising.

'What happened to this temple?' asked the goddess.

'The war,' replied the young woman. She yawned, then smiled as she rose from the couch. 'Have you come to repair it?'

'The Goddess Athena does not go around repairing buildings like a common workman!' cried Bremusa.

'It's cold in winter,' mumbled the girl.

Athena looked around in displeasure. 'Where is the great river spirit Metricia?'

'She was depressed by all the fighting so she changed back into a river and moved away.'

Athena scowled. 'I hate it when you need someone and then you find out they've changed into a river and gone away.'

Nicias

Nicias had been a senior statesman in Athens for too long to take anything for granted, but as the delegates at the peace conference rose for lunch, he felt more than a twinge of optimism. In the past week there had been a great deal of anger, many harsh words, bitter accusations and counter accusations, threats of walkouts and boycotts. Now coming to the fore was the recognition that the war between Athens and Sparta was simply not sustainable. Neither city could go on much longer. For all the intransigence of the Spartan General Acanthus, the belligerence of Athenian General Lamachus, and the rabble-rousing of Hyperbolus, the delegates at the conference were gradually coming round to the view that a treaty had to be agreed. After ten years of fighting, Greece needed a rest.

The Athenian delegates, grey-bearded men with experience of war – one of them old enough to have fought the Persians at Salamis, sixty years ago – were never going to agree with the Spartan contention that the war was their fault, any more than the Spartans were prepared to take responsibility. There was, however, a noticeable movement towards the view that grievances might be put aside and weapons laid down.

Nicias even found himself warming towards General Lamachus. He'd been annoyed with him for months because he was quite sure Lamachus had been putting his own desire for military glory above the best interests of the city. Now, having heard him finally admit in public that perhaps some agreement with the Spartans could be made, Nicias reached out in friendship. They drank a cup of Chian wine together and talked amicably with two Spartan delegates about the last few obstacles in their way. The Megaran trade rights still had to be resolved, and there were prisoner exchanges to be made, but apart from that there didn't seem anything to prevent agreement. As he drank his wine, Nicias made a silent toast to the Goddess

Athena, protector of the city, thanking her for coming to their rescue and bringing peace.

Bremusa

Bremusa glared at the young woman who, she noticed, was wearing a dress that seemed both too fancy and too revealing.

'So when Metricia left you just decided to move into her temple? And spend most of your time drinking, by the looks of it.'

'Hey! I don't drink that much. Maybe an amphora of wine every now and then ... And I didn't move in. I was born here.'

'Born here? Slave? Prostitute? Village idiot?'

The young woman grinned cheerfully. 'I'm Metricia's daughter. Metris, wood nymph, at your service. Or maybe water nymph, depending on the weather. Would you like some wine?'

Bremusa was about to curtly refuse the offer when Athena surprised her by accepting. They sat at a small, rickety wooden table while Metris scooped wine from a large amphora beside her couch, humming cheerfully as she poured it into cups which were not of a suitable quality to be handing to a goddess.

Metris looked about eighteen, though if she was really a nymph, she could be any age. Bremusa didn't take to her at all. She wasn't nearly reverent enough towards the goddess. Handing her a chipped old cup and saying 'It's lovely to meet you, Athena,' was not an appropriate greeting, and her broad grin didn't make it better.

The Goddess Athena remained graceful, even on a tiny wooden stool which had seen better days. 'I regret that Metricia has gone,' said Athena. 'Bremusa here is on her way to Athens. I intended to send Metricia with her.'

'Ooh!' squealed Metris. 'Are you going to the Dionysia? I love the festival. Take me instead!'

Athena stared into her eyes. Metris didn't flinch. She smiled, showing her neat white teeth. She was a pretty young nymph. Bremusa was disliking her more and more.

'I needed Metricia to perform some special tasks in Athens. Do you have your mother's powers?' asked the goddess.

'Absolutely! I have plenty of nymph magic!'

'Then I suppose you might serve in her place.'

The Amazon warrior was moved to protest. 'Goddess, this flighty nymph hardly seems suitable for an important mission. How do we know she's even the river spirit's daughter? She could be anyone. I don't trust her.'

'Bremusa will be pleased to have you along,' said Athena. 'And I'll reward you for good service.'

Nicias

Towards the end of the day's proceedings, Nicias and his companions were strolling round the open courtyard, digesting their meal, sipping wine, refreshing themselves for the final discussions to come, when something odd happened. First, a very strange woman walked by. Nicias had travelled far in his time, but he'd never seen her like. So pale, with such dark eyes. Tall, very beautiful, with her black hair falling over her shoulders, quite unlike any Athenian lady he'd ever seen. Her dress was unusual, some sort of shimmering material, and he couldn't guess where it might have originated. She had a twisted metal emblem hanging from a chain round her neck. Something snake-like, though it was difficult to make out.

Nicias was baffled. Who was she? What was she doing here? From the expressions of the Spartans nearby, she certainly wasn't with them. His only vague guess was that she was some hetaera who'd lost her way, though that seemed improbable. She didn't have the look of a hetaera. Besides, there were hoplites at the gate, and they'd know better than to let a prostitute wander in, no matter how high-class. All eyes were drawn to the mysterious beauty, though no one spoke as she walked by. There was something rather intimidating about her.

Nicias turned to the delegate next to him, to make a comment, but before he could speak, a great argument erupted out of nowhere between the leader of the Spartan delegation, General Acanthus, and Isthmonicus, an Athenian delegate.

'Why should we return Amphipolis to Athens?' demanded the Spartan.

'You'll return it if you ever want to see your precious prisoners again!' yelled Isthmonicus.

'Prisoners taken by treachery!'

'Treachery? The only treachery has been Sparta going behind Athens' back, bribing our allies with Persian gold!'

Nicias was immediately alarmed. This was all territory they'd covered before, at length. These problems were meant to have been solved. Before he could point this out, other voices were raised all round the courtyard as Spartans and Athenians fell to arguing with each other, quite violently. People were yelling, there were accusations of treachery and duplicity, all of them relating to matters that were supposed to have been settled during their discussions.

Nicias looked around hopelessly. The ageing statesman couldn't understand what had happened. It was as if a collective madness had suddenly gripped the peace conference.

Metris, Wood or Water Nymph

Bremusa the Amazon and Metris the nymph began their journey to Athens. It wouldn't take long. The goddess Athena would hasten them on their way, allowing them to cover the distance quickly. Bremusa had never been a talkative woman, and marched in silence. It made her companion's constant chatter all the more annoying.

'It was so exciting to meet the Goddess Athena! It just shows you never can tell what's going to happen. Only yesterday I was telling Pholus the centaur that I was sure things were going to pick up soon, and now I'm going to the festival in Athens!'

Bremusa did not look like a woman on her way to a festival. She carried a long sword on her back and wore leather armour the like of which had not been seen in the world for several hundred years. Around her neck was a necklace made from boars' tusks, something else rarely encountered in the world these days.

Metris waved to a couple of naiads through the trees, then spotted her friend Pholus.

'Hey, Pholus! I'm off on a secret mission for the Goddess Athena!'

The centaur nodded, and looked impressed.

'I'm going to the Dionysia! I'll bring you back something nice!'

'Be quiet,' hissed Bremusa. 'Our mission is secret. No one's meant to know.'

'Pholus won't tell anyone. Maybe a few naiads, no one else. Naiads are quite discreet, when they're sober anyway. It was so exciting meeting Athena! If I succeed on this mission do you think she'll invite me to live on Mount Olympus?'

'No.'

'Not that I don't like my little temple. It's a lovely little temple. But it's sad the way it got ruined in the war.'

They walked on. Metris fingered the small flute that hung daintily around her neck.

'Would I get my own temple?'

'What do you mean?' asked Bremusa.

'If I went to live on Mount Olympus?'

'You're not—'

'A nice big one. With lots of room for statues. I like statues.'

'You're not getting a temple.'

'The goddess said I'd be rewarded. She might invite me to live on Mount Olympus! I suppose I'd have to start being a bit more responsible. But you still have some good times there, right? Drinking, dancing, that sort of thing?'

'Mount Olympus is no concern of yours.'

The nymph wasn't put off by Bremusa's unfriendly tone. She had a lot of questions for her. It wasn't every day that you met someone from the home of the gods.

'What's Zeus really like? Is he scowly like his statues? Or is he more friendly? Did Athena really get born from his head? Is it true she doesn't get on well with Hera? What about Aphrodite? I've always wanted to meet her. Is she really that beautiful? Pholus says she's the most beautiful goddess ever. Is she prettier than Athena? Athena was really pretty.'

Bremusa came to a halt and stared at her companion, rather angrily.

'Be quiet! Stop this inane chatter!'

'Don't you like to talk?'

'No.'

'Oh. I like to talk. Have you ever met Ares the God of War? Is he really fierce? What did Aphrodite see in him? Why are you clutching your brow like that? Are you not feeling well?'

They walked on down the grassy hill. It was a bright, lovely day.

Luxos

As he embarked on his night-time spying mission, Luxos passed by the Altar of Pity, a small, plain altar not far from the agora.

This altar, while not dedicated specifically to any god or goddess, was a popular destination for those in dire need. During the plague, people had gathered there, praying desperately that their gravely ill relatives might recover. These days, mothers could be seen praying for news of their sons missing in battle. Luxos felt a vague desire to offer up a prayer himself, but resisted the urge. His life might not be going that well, but affairs had not yet reached such a crisis. He was still confident that Athena would help him.

He walked west towards the rehearsal space used by Aristophanes' rivals, Eupolis and Leucon. Though the streets were dark, he'd been there often and found it easily enough. Things began to go wrong when he tried to sneak over the fence, caught his tunic and plummeted to the ground, landing painfully. He rose as quickly as he could, and hobbled on. He wasn't certain if there would be a watchman on duty at the rehearsal grounds. Were theatrical props guarded at night? He didn't know but didn't want to be apprehended if they were. Aristophanes had given him enough money for a few good meals, and he was pleased about that, but he didn't want to be caught trying to measure phalluses. It would be bad for his reputation which, Luxos acknowledged, was already poor. The young poet was not generally regarded as a valuable member of Athenian society.

He felt a twinge of sadness. *I shouldn't have to be doing this. I'm a poet. I'm not cut out for secret missions. I never claimed to be any good as a spy.*

He peered into several dark huts, looking for theatrical props. Why was Aristophanes so worried about penises for his chorus anyway?

You wouldn't catch a real poet worrying about that, thought Luxos. *I could entertain the Athenians without a lot of funny props if someone would just give me a chance.* But they're all such a mean clique, the poets and their friends. They won't listen

36

to me. They wouldn't read my poems even if I could afford to get copies made.

Athens' most successful poets had their work copied onto scrolls and widely distributed, but that was expensive. Without a wealthy sponsor, Luxos's poetry was never going to find its way into the best Athenian households.

The light from the moon was fairly bright and Luxos was still worried about being caught, but there didn't seem to be any sort of security. Presumably Athens had more than enough worries at the moment without assigning valuable citizens the task of guarding props.

There they are. Luxos eased his way into one of the huts and started rummaging around among several sacks full of comedy stage-penises.

They do seem quite big.

Aristophanes had asked Luxos to measure them. That was difficult in the dark wooden hut. After a few minutes' frustration, he loaded himself up with as many as he could carry, draping them over his shoulders and arms, and went back outside. There, in the bright moonlight, he walked straight into the most beautiful girl in the whole world. Or so it seemed to Luxos. There was also an intimidating woman with a sword.

The most beautiful girl in the world had big brown eyes and long black wavy hair. She wore a short white dress and delicate little sandals. Luxos stared at her in awe. For the first time in living memory, he couldn't think of anything to say. He did realise that he was draped in a great bundle of funny phalluses. He regretted that. It seemed to be hindering conversation.

There was a long silence. Finally the intimidating-looking woman turned to her young companion.

'I told you Athenians were obsessed with penises.'

With that they walked off. Luxos gazed after them, awestruck at the girl's other-worldly beauty. He knew he was in love.

Aristophanes

In the early morning light, Aristophanes was so wrapped up in bitter thoughts about his producer that he almost tumbled into the open sewer that ran past the statue of Solon the Wise. He avoided it at the last moment, only to bump into Nicias, also engrossed in his own thoughts. Aristophanes knew Nicias quite well, though the politician came from an older generation. He held him in reasonable esteem, regarding him as honest, if uninspired. Aristophanes had rarely mocked him in his comedies, and when he had, the ridicule had not been too severe. There had been one memorable scene in which the actor playing Nicias made such a boring speech that the entire assembly fell asleep. The real Nicias hadn't made a fuss about it, acknowledging that he'd never been Athens' most gifted orator, although privately he'd been rather offended by it.

'Nicias. Shouldn't you be wringing concessions from the Spartans?'

Nicias shook his head wearily. 'The conference broke up.'

'Broke up? How?'

'In chaos. It was all I could do to prevent a brawl between the delegates. If I hadn't got General Lamachus out of there he'd be facing an impiety charge for murdering a guest in our city.'

'How could that happen? Everyone said it was going well.'

Nicias spread his hands hopelessly. Aristophanes noticed he was looking older. Soon his actors would need a new funny mask to represent him.

'I don't know how it happened. One minute we were close to agreement, the next a frightful row broke out. Everyone was accusing everyone else of lies and treachery, and every agreement we'd made was being torn up and trampled in the dust. I've never seen anything like it.'

Nicias looked around at the small boys trotting along behind their tutors, the men pushing their carts of olives towards the market.

'Aristophanes, have you noticed anything strange recently?'

'Like what?'

'I don't know exactly ... But people are starting to act oddly. It's like there's something in the air. Something bad.'

'Ten years of war will do that.'

'I know, but ...' Nicias gazed wistfully at the statues of Harmodius and Aristogeiton, in front of the law court at the edge of the agora. The city could do with more heroes like them. 'People are acting out of character. It's like the plague all over again.'

Aristophanes shuddered. It wasn't that long since the terrible disease had ravaged Athens: only six or seven years since the last outbreak. They had been grim years, and he knew what Nicias meant about citizens acting out of character. There had been times, when the dead were strewn around unburied in the streets, and the dying lay helpless and alone in their houses, when all normal standards of decent behaviour seemed to have deserted Athens.

'Please, Nicias, I saw my parents die. I don't like to remember it. Things aren't that bad yet.'

'No, it's not that bad. But it's heading that way. Half the people I've talked to today seem to have taken leave of their senses.' Nicias shook his head. 'Maybe it is just the war. I hope your play is going well?'

Aristophanes shrugged, not wanting to describe his many theatrical worries. Nicias, however, seemed unusually interested in his progress, and pressed his enquiry.

'It might be very helpful if you put on a great comedy dedicated to peace.'

'Do you really think so?'

'Certainly.'

Aristophanes was flattered. He'd never heard an important politician imply that his comedies might be of any importance. He regretted that he couldn't give Nicias better news.

'To be honest, it's not going well. In fact we're close to disaster.'

'A successful comedy promoting peace might be just what Athens needs at this moment.'

'I know. But it's still a disaster.'

Bremusa

Bremusa had excellent night vision. It was an Amazon trait. Even as the moon began to disappear behind the clouds, she successfully avoided the pitfalls of the Athenian streets, guiding herself and Metris to the foot of the acropolis.

'This should do, we're close to the centre of the city. Time for you to act.'

Metris looked blank. 'Act? Am I meant to act?'

'I mean it's time for you to locate Laet.'

The nymph continued to look blank.

'Find Laet. That's what the goddess sent you here for.'

'Right.' Metris looked at her sandals. She had small, delicate feet.

'Well?' Bremusa grew impatient. 'Use your nymph magic to locate her.'

There was a long silence.

'You do have powers of locating, don't you? Like your mother?'

'Well . . . not exactly,' said Metris.

'What do you mean "not exactly"? You said you had your mother's gifts.'

'I didn't inherit absolutely all of them.'

Bremusa glared at Metris. 'Are you telling me you can't magically locate her?'

'I'm afraid not.'

'If we can't even find Laet, how can you use your soothing nymph-powers to dispel her negative energy?'

The nymph shifted uncomfortably under Bremusa's glare. 'About that ...' She looked up. 'Oh look, you can just see the Parthenon. Isn't it lovely?'

'Never mind the Parthenon! Are you telling me you can't dispel negative energy?'

'Not for powerful beings like Laet, no. Though I'm good with children. And cats always like me.'

'Don't talk to me about children and cats! You were sent here to perform a task and now you can't do it! Have you been lying about everything?'

'Of course not. You might just have got the wrong impression about a few things.'

Bremusa growled in frustration. 'You can't do the things you were brought here for! That's not a wrong impression! That's you making things up. I don't believe you're even the daughter of a river spirit. You probably just made that up too.'

'I did not! I was Metricia's favourite daughter. Second favourite. Third at the very least.'

Bremusa glared at her in the way she'd once glared at enemies on the battlefield. 'Did you inherit any of your mother's powers?'

'Of course!'

'Like what?'

'I can make daisies and buttercups grow really quickly. Look!'

Metris waved her hand. Quite magically, a host of daisies and buttercups appeared at their feet. Standing amongst a small sea of flowers, the nymph seemed pleased with herself.

'Aren't they lovely?'

'Lovely? Is that your only power? What use is that to anyone?'

Metris smiled cheerfully. 'It always brightens things up.'

'You idiot! No one cares about buttercups and daisies! That's

41

not going to save Athens. Why did you lie about your powers?'

'I wanted to come to the festival ... it's draughty in my temple since it got ruined.'

'I'll ruin you, you—'

The Amazon broke off as four Scythian archers walked by; the night patrol, keeping order in the city. They looked over suspiciously, though their expressions softened when Metris smiled at them and gave them a cheerful wave.

'The Goddess Athena is not going to be pleased with you,' said Bremusa, when the archers had gone.

That didn't seem to worry Metris. By now her attention had wandered to other matters. 'I wonder why that young man was carrying all those penises?'

'Probably because he was the local idiot.'

'I thought he looked nice. Did you notice how nice his hair was? And he had nice eyes too.'

'Stop saying "nice". Nothing about him was nice.'

'I hope we meet him again. He looked nice.'

Aristophanes and Luxos

Aristophanes was trying to sort out some problems in the chorus's second-act choreography when young Luxos bounded into the rehearsal space, looking eager. Aristophanes left the chorus in the hands of Hermogenes and went over to talk to him.

'Stop grinning at me in that offensive manner. What happened on your mission?'

'I measured both your rivals' phalluses. Leucon and Eupolis's are much bigger. Good working order too, from what I could see. There'll be some mighty erections on stage when they get going. Might be some sort of new record.'

The playwright scowled. It was bad news. Their producers

were providing them with enough money for props, despite the hardships in Athens.

'It's because their plays are so bland. They get money because they never offend anyone. Damn them.'

Aristophanes hunted around for some coins to pay Luxos for his work. He noticed the young poet was still smiling. Aristophanes, burdened by worry, found this mildly irritating.

'What are you so happy about?'

'I'm in love.'

'You're always in love.'

'This time it's the real thing!' gushed Luxos.

Aristophanes' irritation increased. As if Luxos's unceasing attempts to break into the refined world of Athenian poetry weren't annoying enough, he was always falling in love as well, and he liked to talk about it.

'Weren't you already in love with Phryne the courtesan?'

'That was only a passing fancy.'

'You wrote a hundred-line elegy to her.'

Luxos brushed this aside. 'I may have felt some temporary attraction. But this is the real thing. She's the most beautiful girl in Athens!'

'Really? How much does she charge?'

'She's not a courtesan!'

'What's her name?'

Luxos looked confused. 'Eh ... '

'Where's she from?'

'Eh ... '

'Did you even talk to her?'

'No,' admitted Luxos. 'But we shared some significant eye contact. I tell you, it's the real thing.'

There is the heat of Love,
the pulsing rush of Longing, the lover's whisper,
irresistible – magic to make the sanest man go mad.

'I've never thought you were that sane, Luxos. And don't quote Homer at me.'

Aristophanes looked down at Luxos, who was not tall. At the sight of his smiling face, his shaggy blond hair and eager blue eyes, he felt his irritation growing. Athens was suffering and this young fool was going around smiling, telling people he was in love with a girl he'd never even spoken to.

'Shouldn't you be doing something useful, like rowing a trireme?'

'Can I bring her to Callias's symposium?'

'Of course not. Can't you get it into your head you're not invited? If you show up at Callias's drinking party he'll have you brutalised by the Scythian archers.'

'But she's really pretty. I'm sure you'd like her. And I can recite my poetry while I'm there.'

'Enough, Luxos. I need to see the prop-maker and get him to make our phalluses bigger somehow.'

'Are they really that important?'

'Of course. If Eupolis has bigger and funnier penises, why would the jury vote for my play?'

'Because they'd still be in a good mood after I'd recited some great poetry before your play! Let me have that spot, it'll really help you.'

'I've already asked Isidoros.'

'Isidoros?' Luxos was aghast. 'He's an awful poet.'

'He's popular.'

'That doesn't mean he's any good.'

There was something in that, but Aristophanes had had enough. He had too many problems to indulge Luxos's flights of fancy. Already he could see his rivals being lauded at the festival while he was disparaged. Mocked, even. His plays had brought him many enemies. They'd like nothing better than to see him mount a shabby production and be derided by the audience. The Athenian audience could be very critical. The rough proletarian mass of Athenian oarsmen would not stand for an inferior comedy. Fruit and vegetables had been thrown. Aristophanes' blood ran cold at the thought of his chorus being pelted with fruit.

The sun was climbing rapidly. The sheltered rehearsal space would soon be baking hot.

'Luxos. I almost admire your ambition. And your relentless optimism. But can't you understand that no one in Athens is ever going to listen to your poetry? You don't come from the right class. You weren't educated like a gentleman. You never had a proper teacher. You don't have a patron, or any influential friends. Give it up. It's hopeless. It'll only make you unhappy. Here's the money I owe you. Now go back to the docks where you belong, and try and make something of your life there.'

For the first time, Luxos seemed to understand what Aristophanes was saying. The light in his eyes dimmed a little. Aristophanes handed him his money, then returned to his choreography.

Bremusa

There was a small shrine close to the harbour, rarely used, through which Bremusa could communicate with the goddess. Furious with Metris for her lies, the Amazon left her trailing in her wake as she hurried towards Piraeus.

What am I going to do now? Metris was meant to locate Laet, and then dispel her bad energy. It turns out she can't do either. I knew she was an impostor.

Their plan having failed at the first obstacle, Bremusa had no idea how to proceed. She'd fought in many battles but she'd never been a good tactician. Generally she'd left strategy to others. She turned left at a crossroads marked by the Herm

45

statues that were everywhere in Athens. Little square columns, with a head and a penis. She wondered if Messenger God Hermes liked them.

I'll have to ask him next time I see him.

The road to the unused shrine ran over a rough area of shingle next to the shore, vacant save for some children playing in the distance. Bremusa halted to take her bearings, trying to remember the directions Athena had given her.

'Hello, Bremusa,' came a male voice. Bremusa jumped. Having left the mortal realm hundreds of years ago, she hadn't been expecting anyone to address her by name. She spun round to find herself staring at a man she'd never forgotten, or forgiven. A tall, sturdy man, with a black beard, wearing a bronze breastplate of a design which had not been seen in this world for a very long time.

'Idomeneus!'

He bowed. 'Indeed. Idomeneus of Crete. I never thought I'd meet you again, Bremusa of the Amazons. How long has it been?'

Bremusa placed her hand on the pommel of her sword, watching him warily. 'Almost eight hundred years.'

'Really? Is it that long since the war at Troy?' Idomeneus laughed. He had a deep, earthy, intimidating voice. 'You managed to flee just before I killed you.'

'I've never fled from battle, Idomeneus of Crete.'

They stared at each other, both in their archaic armour, on a quiet rocky beach, relics from the past.

'What are you doing here? And how have you lived so long?'

Idomeneus drew his sword. 'I could ask you the same. But I think I'd rather just finish what I started at Troy.'

Bremusa drew her sword. Idomeneus stepped forward, and they fought. On Olympus, Bremusa had not neglected her training, but she'd had few occasions to use a sword in anger. Growing up as a young Amazon warrior, she was fighting all

46

the time. Her life depended on it. These days, she wasn't as sharp.

Idomeneus had been a commander, a man who led his troops into battle. He'd killed many opponents. He'd even engaged in combat with the mighty Hector, and lived to tell of it. He was a fearless and skilful warrior. He forced Bremusa back. The shingle beneath their feet was poor footing, shifting and sliding as she desperately parried each of his thrusts. Unlike their ancient encounter before the walls of Troy, neither of them carried shields, making their fight even more hazardous. Bremusa knew she couldn't allow him close. His blade, swung with such strength, would cut right through her leather armour. It didn't need to be a lethal blow; a wounding strike would be enough to create an opening for him to kill her.

Though she was forced back, the Amazon felt no fear. In battle, she never had. Hard-pressed as she was, she still looked for opportunities to attack, and her blade almost made it through Idomeneus's defence, making him pause. His expression changed as he remembered that Bremusa the Amazon was also a dangerous opponent.

Bremusa was a tall woman, but Idomeneus towered over her. As she stepped backwards, parrying another stroke, she felt her heel brush against an overturned rowing boat. She'd noticed this before, and was expecting it. She nimbly hopped backwards onto the wooden boat, raising her eighteen inches or so and giving her a height advantage. When Idomeneus rushed forward she slashed downwards with all her might. Her blade almost evaded his guard and actually cut into his beard. Idomeneus, uninjured but humiliated, roared with anger and attacked even more violently. At that moment, the rotting timbers of the elderly rowing boat gave way and Bremusa sprawled backwards onto the stony beach.

Her situation was now desperate. She was close to death on several occasions as she struggled to rise while blocking her opponent's sword. She'd almost made it back to her feet when they were interrupted by a woman's laugh. It wouldn't have made Bremusa stop fighting but, to her surprise, Idomeneus took a step backwards. He didn't lower his guard, but did turn his eyes to the newcomer. Bremusa risked a sidelong glance. She realised she no longer had to search for Laet. The female who strolled to Idomeneus's side could be no one else, because she was obviously not quite human.

Laet was tall, like the Amazon. Her robe was as finely spun as anything seen on Mount Olympus, but darker, and it clung to her figure in a way that might have made Aphrodite envious. She glanced at the broken timbers.

'You shouldn't have jumped on that old boat. The timbers were bound to give way. But people do seem to make bad decisions when I'm around.'

She turned to Idomeneus. 'Idomeneus, we're trying to remain discreet. Is it necessary for you to fight this woman?'

'She's an Amazon. I hate Amazons. I'd have killed her at Troy, if she hadn't suddenly vanished when my spear was at her throat.'

'Really?' Laet regarded Bremusa with her coal-black eyes. The pallor of her skin suggested she was rarely exposed to sunlight, or even daylight.

'You fought at Troy?'

'I did.'

'But you disappeared from the field of battle? Presumably you were saved by some god?'

'By the Goddess Athena.'

'Ah. I see. Have you been with her ever since?'

'Yes.'

'Then I assume the goddess has now sent you here to look for me?'

That, thought Bremusa, *was rather astute*. Not wanting to show she was impressed by her deduction, she didn't reply.

'No doubt Athena fears I'll wreck the peace conference.' Laet smiled, not pleasantly. 'She's right.'

Incongruously, she yawned. Bremusa felt insulted.

'Come, Idomeneus. I'm tired. There are children playing nearby and that always gives me a headache. I don't find this Amazon very interesting. You can kill her another time if it really bothers you.'

They walked off up the shingle beach towards the city. Bremusa watched them go. She suddenly realised how fatigued she was from the battle, under the sun, in her leather armour. Her skin was caked with perspiration.

Two children ran screaming in front of her, pursued by their female attendant. She was a stern-looking woman who scolded her charges, both around eight years old.

'Plato, Xenophon, stop fighting! Can't you behave better in public? Stop staring at the foreign woman and come with me.'

They departed, young Plato and Xenophon still scuffling with each other. Bremusa turned round and hurried towards the shrine. She urgently needed to talk to the Goddess Athena.

Luxos

There were two shops in Athens which sold beautiful, expensive lyres, instruments good enough for a professional to play on stage. There were several stalls in the agora that stocked instruments of slightly lesser quality, the sort that wealthy young men might use while for playing music with their friends. Close to the harbour, there was Straton's junk shop which sold the cheapest instruments in the city. That was where Luxos had bought his lyre. It wasn't a high-quality instrument. He wasn't even sure that it was made from genuine turtle shell. Nonetheless, Luxos loved his lyre, and had taught himself to play, copying the musicians he saw performing at the gymnasium. A true Greek poet recited his poetry to the accompaniment of the lyre, and Luxos had learned how to do it, without instruction.

Not far from the junk shop was Lysander's pawn shop, current location of Luxos's lyre. He'd been ashamed when he pawned it to buy food; as ashamed as a man throwing down his shield when he fled from the battlefield: he'd only done it after fainting from hunger. Like many people in Athens, Luxos was very poor, and unlike most, he had no family to fall back on. As a young orphan the community, his deme, had fed and cared for him, after a fashion, but after he reached the age of eighteen he was on his own. It would have been difficult at the best of times. With Athens in the state it now was, he was struggling to survive. For a while he'd tried to earn money by singing and playing on the street, but no citizen in Piraeus had much money to spare for street performers. He tried playing in some of the wealthier areas uptown, but the Scythian archers chased him away.

Now, with Aristophanes' money, he hurried to reclaim his lyre. He was happy and excited to retrieve his instrument, but as he left the shop, he remembered what Aristophanes had said. No one would ever listen to his songs or his poetry. Previously Luxos had ignored all criticism, banished all discouragement, but for some reason the words struck home. He looked around at Athens, and for the first time it seemed like an unfriendly place. There was something different in the air. He couldn't say what, but he could feel a great cloud of depression settling over him.

Luxos the poet trudged home, to the abandoned shack behind the great dockyard where triremes were constructed. There he sat and played his lyre. This cheered him a little, but he kept hearing Aristophanes' words: *You don't come from the right class. You weren't educated like a gentleman. You never had a proper teacher. You don't have a patron, or any influential friends.* It was all true. The sons of the wealthy citizens of Athens were schooled in literature, philosophy and rhetoric from a young age. Luxos wasn't. Those same wealthy young men had influential friends to call upon should they ever wish to see their lyrics or poetry performed in public. Luxos knew no one influential.

His shoulders slumped. For as long as he could remember, he'd dreamed of striding out onto the stage at the great theatre and performing for the whole of Athens. Now he wondered if that would ever happen. Perhaps Aristophanes was right. Perhaps no one would ever be interested in his poetry.

Aristophanes

Aristophanes knew that Philippus wasn't happy. He was a good actor but he'd never been able to reconcile himself to being successful only in comedies. He could put a funny line over like few others in Athens, but somewhere in his mind there was the thought that, really, he should have been a serious dramatic player, taking the leading role in one of the great tragedies of Sophocles or Aeschylus. Aristophanes found it difficult to sympathise. It wasn't as if being a successful comic actor hadn't brought Philippus success. He'd won plaudits on numerous occasions, in his plays, and in others'. People still talked of his hilarious performance in Aristophanes' production last year, *The Wasps*. He had plenty of admirers, and a good reputation throughout the city. It should have been enough, in Aristophanes' opinion.

Actors. They're never satisfied with what they have.

It was no surprise when Hermogenes told him that Philippus was complaining.

'He's always complaining. What's wrong this time? Not enough olives in his dressing room?'

'It's the dung beetle. He doesn't like it.'

Aristophanes followed Hermogenes across to the rehearsal

stage where Philippus, in mask and costume, was sitting astride a giant dung beetle. This beetle was one of their few successful props, constructed to look rather humorous. It was brightly painted, with a smiling expression and a fat, funny body. By means of the stage crane, it could be hoisted into the air and made to fly over the stage. It could even be swung over the front rows of the audience, which was quite a spectacular effect. When Philippus used his giant phallus as a rudder to steer the flying beetle, it was going to get a huge laugh. Even the stagehands found it funny, and they were generally a hard group to please, having already seen most things.

Philippus slipped his mask up over his head. 'Aristophanes! Are you sure this scene is necessary?'

'It's our big opening.'

'I don't like it.'

'Why not?'

'It's undignified.'

'I wouldn't say that.'

'I'm flying a gigantic dung beetle!' cried Philippus. 'How much more undignified could it be?' He glared down at the playwright. 'I am a serious actor, you know.'

'You're flying up to heaven to ask the gods to end the war. What could be more serious than that?'

The scene was a parody of the well-known story of the hero flying to heaven on the winged horse Pegasus. Aristophanes' play started off with Philippus feeding the beetle more and more dung, till it was large enough for him to mount. His family questioned his sanity, but Philippus claimed to be the sanest person in Athens. He was sick of the war, and he planned to visit the gods, and ask them to end it.

'Pegasus flying to heaven was serious,' said Philippus. 'This is farcical.'

'Exactly!' cried Aristophanes. 'But I'm not really getting it from your performance. Try pulling on your phallus a little more when you're steering. Get it waving around so the audience can see it.'

He left Philippus muttering about the time he'd been the lead actor in *Oedipus*, and what a mistake it had been to ever get involved with the crude comedies of Aristophanes.

'He's always the same,' said Aristophanes to his assistant. 'Always wants to be taken seriously.'

'He'll be fine once the crowd starts applauding. That always works like magic. Did you manage to squeeze any more money out of our choregos?'

'I'm afraid not. Antimachus won't cough up.'

Hermogenes shook his head. He was a few years older than Aristophanes, and he'd been in the theatre all his life. 'It's unusual for a producer to starve his production of funds. Being chosen as choregos is meant to be an honour.'

'That's what I told him, but it was no use. He's still annoyed because I mildly lampooned him on stage.'

'You grossly insulted him,' said Hermogenes.

'I wasn't to know he had no sense of humour. I've grossly insulted most important men in the city, they don't normally hold a grudge.

'Kleon prosecuted you.'

Aristophanes scowled. That had been quite an affair. The leader of the pro-war faction had taken his revenge by prosecuting him for impiety. The playwright had been fined, and it could have been worse.

'I'm sorry to say this about a fellow Athenian citizen, but I was relieved when he was killed last year.'

'You weren't the only one,' said Hermogenes.

Many people thought that with Kleon gone, it might be easier to bring the war to an end, particularly as Brasidas, the Spartan war-leader, had also died in battle.

'I really thought we'd make peace when they were both killed,' said Aristophanes. 'It was a great opportunity. But there seems to be no limit on how foolish the citizens of Athens can be. Kleon was a warmonger but Hyperbolus is even worse. Why do people listen to these demagogues?'

They paused for a while to watch the chorus go through the dance steps that introduced the last act of the play. Aristophanes had choreographed a very funny sequence involving a lot of phallus twirling, none of which seemed to be working out very well. The chorus was often a problem. They weren't professionals, just honest citizens recruited for the festival. It often took some time to whip them into shape.

'I think there's more to it than just Antimachus hating me. He told me that certain important people don't want me writing a play that promotes peace.'

'I can guess who these certain important people are.' Hermogenes frowned as two members of the chorus got their dance steps wrong and collided with each other. 'Are you sure you want to insult Hyperbolus in this play? He'll be in the audience with his supporters. It could lead to trouble.'

'Hyperbolus is scum. He needs to be insulted.'

'I wouldn't exactly say that he was scum,' said Hermogenes.

'I can't believe you're still defending him!' cried Aristophanes.

'I come from a family of sailors. We've always supported the democratic faction.'

'Can't you see he's nothing more than a self-serving loudmouth?'

'I can see that he helped distribute food to the poor when the rich men of Athens weren't doing much to help.'

Aristophanes and Hermogenes glared at each other. The argument might have gone further had not both realised that the last thing they needed was more friction in the rehearsal room.

'Just keep me out of the court case. I have four children to support.'

Aristophanes didn't know Hermogenes had four children. He had a vague memory he might have been at the birth celebrations for some of them.

Metris

Metris had admitted to Bremusa that she didn't have the ability to locate anyone. That was true, as far as the nymph knew. There was no real reason that she should. Her mother had been a powerful being, but these powers were not always passed down. The world of the semi-divines – the cult heroes, spirits, nymphs, centaurs and all the rest – was not known to run on any logical system. Despite her supposed lack of power, Metris didn't have any trouble locating Luxos. She could sense his presence. She walked south, down through the long walls, towards the port at Piraeus. Though keen to find him, she paused on her way to admire the Athenian statues, of which there were many. Metris loved the statues. They were vibrant, lifelike, imposing, and brightly coloured. All the best Greek sculptors had worked here.

Near the harbour, the surroundings were less pleasant. There were beggars on the streets and the air smelled of rotting fish. The houses were small and ramshackle, and what temples there were seemed badly in need of repair.

Metris spotted Luxos sitting on a small hillock. She smiled at the sight of his thick, tousled hair. Who had hair like that? No one she'd ever seen. She could sense his sadness. He was playing his lyre, and though his playing didn't quite compare with the music of the water nymphs, which was so beautiful it could lure a man to his death, it was heartfelt and moving. Metris could see the sad aura emanating from Luxos as he sat on his own on the dusty ground. She walked up to him and laid her hand on his shoulder. His tunic was so threadbare she could feel his skin through the fabric.

'You're sad.'

He nodded. 'No one will listen to my poetry.'

She sat down beside him. 'I'll listen.'

'Really?'

Metris had never seen such a dilapidated lyre. It was nothing like the fine instruments of the water nymphs. But the young poet knew how to play it. He recited a rather sad poem about the loss of a parent, accompanying his words with a few gentle notes.

'What's your name?' asked Metris, after he'd finished.

'Luxos.'

'I'm Metris.'

Quite abruptly, she kissed him. The air grew warm, and a great carpet of buttercups and daisies blanketed the hillock.

'I like your poetry.'

'I like your flowers.'

Metris took a strand of his funny blond hair in her fingers. 'Who could resist your poetry?'

'The whole of Athens. Aristophanes says I'm not the right sort of person. I just realised he's probably correct.'

Luxos had such a pretty face. Metris had never seen such a pretty youth.

'I wouldn't mind so much, but I'd like to have been given a chance before I get killed in battle.'

'Battle?' Metris was surprised. 'Surely you don't go to war?'

'Everyone in Athens goes to war. Farmers, philosophers, carpenters, poets – everyone. The order comes out, you turn up with three days' rations, and off you go.'

'I can't imagine you in battle. What's it like?'

Luxos looked very troubled. 'Terrible,' he said, and didn't seem inclined to describe it further.

'Couldn't you refuse to fight?'

The young poet was shocked by the suggestion. 'Athens needs everyone. I might be feeble but I'm not a coward. I do my best, even if I'm not much use at it.'

Metris put her face close to his and looked into his blue eyes. 'My warrior hero,' she said, and kissed him again.

After a few moments, she rose daintily to her feet. She knew that Bremusa would be looking for her.

'I have to go now. But I'll find you again.'

Aristophanes

Aristophanes sat on a couch with Theodota, in her stately villa in the west side of town, home to all the city's most successful hetaerae. At twenty-four, Theodota was Athens' most beautiful and most famous courtesan. Aristophanes lusted after her permanently, and quite painfully. He desperately wished that she liked him more. The playwright had given her a lot of money in the past year. It hadn't made much difference. They sat next to each other comfortably enough, but no one would have said they were intimate. Finely wrought earrings of delicate gold, imported from Syracuse, hung seductively on the courtesan's ears, a present from Aristophanes, given to her only the day before. Theodota loved the earrings: she showed no sign of loving Aristophanes.

He watched as her young female servant Mnesarete poured wine for them.

'To your beauty,' he said, toasting Theodota.

'To Athens,' said Theodota.

Aristophanes had come here for a purpose other than simply lust, but once again, Theodota was not responding as well as he'd hoped.

'Why won't you do it?'

'I'm afraid it's out of the question, Aristophanes.'

'Why?'

'I have my reputation to consider.'

That seemed like an unsatisfactory answer. 'Reputation? Theodota, you're Athens' most famous courtesan.'

'Exactly. Why would men pay for my services if they could already see me walking around naked for free?'

'It would really help me out.'

'I still don't see why you need a woman to come on stage at the end of your play and walk around naked. Isn't that a little cheap?'

'Cheap? You're as bad as Hermogenes with his artistic principles. I'm not Aeschylus, you know. I'm not writing a great tragedy. I'm writing a comedy and I'm trying to win the prize for it, which means impressing a panel of judges. Five men drawn by lot, who for some reason always turn out to be the five most ignorant men in the city. And nothing would impress these ignorant judges more than Athens' most beautiful woman walking out naked on stage.'

'Isn't female nudity against festival rules?'

'We'll give you a few pieces of string.'

Theodota laughed. When she laughed, her features lit up. It was intoxicating, even more intoxicating than her voice, which was already enough to hypnotise most of the men with whom she came into contact.

'Sorry, Aristophanes, I'm not doing it. The Athenians don't mind me plying my trade here as long as I'm reasonably discreet, but if I start wandering around naked at the Dionysia I'll be in trouble.'

'I think you might be more helpful, Theodota. I'm really struggling.'

'Everyone's finding it difficult these days, with the war.'

Aristophanes grunted with annoyance. 'My rivals don't seem to be suffering. They've got decent producers. Damn Eupolis and Leucon. Neither of them can write to save their lives. All you get from them is one cheap stunt after another. Are you sure you won't appear naked?'

Theodota sipped her wine. She wore an expression Aristophanes had come to recognise, an expression that meant he wasn't going to get what he wanted.

'You could ask someone else. Mnesarete, for instance. She's pretty. Good figure too.'

'Your maid? It wouldn't be the same.' Aristophanes' face clouded over. 'I bet you'd do it for Socrates.'

Theodota rolled her eyes. 'Not this again.'

He felt a familiar bad temper coming on. 'Well, you obviously like him better than me.'

'I'm not having a relationship with Socrates.'

'You would if he asked. You probably wouldn't even charge him. Why are all the courtesans in Athens so keen on Socrates?'

'Why?' said Theodota. 'I suppose it's because he's intelligent and funny, and he gives good advice. He's nice to us and treats us with respect. And he doesn't want anything from us in return.'

'Yes, fine. I wasn't really looking for such a detailed answer.'

Aristophanes scowled, angered at the injustice of it. Theodota was capable of freezing out anyone she didn't like. Her regal disdain could leave a man feeling crushed. There were famous, handsome, wealthy Athenians she'd never accept as clients, because she'd taken a dislike to them for some reason. But whenever shabby, ugly, old Socrates appeared, she just fawned over him like a little girl. It was infuriating. Damn Socrates. Aristophanes felt glad he'd made fun of him in his last play.

Idomeneus

Idomeneus entered the room upstairs in the tavern and placed a heavy bag of silver on the table.

'I have the money from Euphranor.'

'Is it all there?'

'Minus the priestess's commission.'

'Ah, the priestess. How is Kleonike?'

'A lot wealthier since she started accepting bribes. I get the impression some of the group that hired her aren't too pleased at the amount she charges.'

Laet's lips twitched in the semblance of a smile. 'Then they're fools. Kleonike is worth it to them. She's worth more. There aren't that many mortals left who can summon a semi-divine.'

Idomeneus looked at her quizzically. 'You've been summoned by a lot of priestesses in your time.'

'I have. But mostly in the centuries after Troy. Have you not noticed the amount of human contact lessening, these recent years?'

Idomeneus shrugged. 'I suppose so. I never gave it much thought.'

'The days of close connection between Mount Olympus and the cities of Greece are coming to an end, Idomeneus. Heroes no longer walk with men. Centaurs no longer teach the sons of kings. The divines are withdrawing, and the semi-divines are following them. Kleonike is one of the last priestesses capable of making contact with us.' Laet looked thoughtful. 'That woman on the beach. It's a surprise to find an Amazon in Athens. Apparently the Goddess Athena has not yet relinquished direct intervention.'

She took a coin from the bag and examined it. 'Best quality silver. The mines at Laurium have always been very beneficial for Athens. If not for the slaves who have to dig it out the ground.'

'What do you care about their slaves?'

'Nothing at all. Though I'm amused at these philosophers talking about ethics when it's wealth from their slaves that keeps them prosperous.'

Laet put the coin in her purse, an elegantly embroidered item from Corinth. 'It's so gratifying to be paid for spreading destruction. Often I've done it for free.'

'I hear the peace conference almost came to blows.'

'It's not hard to spread disorder among people who already hate each other. The Athenians and Spartans are locked into their ways and will never change. It will finish them eventually.'

Laet looked around the small tavern room, which was clean but furnished in very basic fashion.

'You must rent us a house somewhere. I don't like this tavern.'

She gazed out of the window, northwards to the fine white

buildings and marble columns of Athens. She murmured a line from Euripides' *Medea*:

> *I'll travel to the land of Erechtheus,*
> *to live with Aegeus, son of Pandion.*

'Which reminds me, Idomeneus, I'd like to go to the theatre.'
'The theatre? What for?'
'I'm a cultured woman.'
'Are you planning on spreading some reckless folly around?'
'That depends on whether or not I like the plays.'

The Goddess Athena

On Mount Olympus, the Goddess Athena was impatient. She took a cup of wine from an attendant, but held it in front of her without drinking.

'What's keeping Bremusa? She should have reported by now.'

The goddess was monitoring one of the altars in her mansion. It was directly connected to the small shrine near the harbour in Athens.

'There's someone entering the shrine now,' said her attendant. As they watched, the door to the rather small, dark space opened.

'Finally,' said the goddess. 'Open it up so Bremusa can see me through the altar there.'

The figure lit a candle.

'It's not Bremusa!' cried the goddess. 'It's that idiotic young poet! Quickly, close it down! Don't let him see me.'

The attendant hurriedly spoke a few words, lowering a mystical barrier, ensuring that Luxos could not see all the way to Olympus. Unaware that he was being observed by Athena,

Luxos faced the altar in front of him and bowed to the small statue of the goddess.

On Mount Olympus, Athena frowned. 'I hope this doesn't go on too long. I want to talk to Bremusa.'

Luxos was talking quite animatedly. '. . . and I wrote this great piece of lyric poetry which would fit right into the final scene of Aristophanes' play but he won't even listen to it! And then I asked if I could read some of my poetry before his play starts, because that's a really good spot, the whole of Athens would hear me. I've got some new metrical innovations which would really shake things up. I could revolutionise poetry in Athens! But Aristophanes says that spot is reserved for a well-known poet so he's giving it to Isidoros. I'd be much better than him! And then I asked if I could come to his drinking party because all these wealthy people will be there that might want to sponsor me but he says I can't come. Aristophanes is really mean . . . He could help me get my poetry heard if he wanted.'

There was a pause.

'But that's not really why I came to talk to you tonight, Goddess.'

'There's more?' sighed Athena.

'I met this wonderful girl! She's beautiful and nice and friendly and she likes my poetry and everything! But of course I didn't have any money to buy her food or anything, because I'm so poor. But she didn't seem to mind. She was so lovely. I was wondering if you could help me find her again, and maybe put in a good word for me? I think she might be some sort of nymph. Well, she was good at making daisies anyway. I really need to find her again.'

At that moment, as the goddess and her attendant watched, Bremusa poked her head into the shrine.

'Are you going to be in there all night? Other people want to pray, you know!'

'Hey,' cried Luxos. 'Don't interrupt other people's prayers. It's

62

impious. Oh, wait, you're the woman that was with Metris! Are you her friend? Is she here now? Wow, I've never had a prayer answered so quickly!'

Luxos turned eagerly back towards the altar. 'You brought her here already! Thank you, Goddess Athena. Look, I brought you some daisies!'

With that Luxos rushed from the small shrine. Back on Mount Olympus, Athena's attendant was raising an eyebrow.

'Daisies?'

'It's all he can afford,' said the goddess, rather stiffly.

'No chance of him roasting an ox, I suppose.'

Inside the shrine, Bremusa was looking a little flustered. She hadn't expected Luxos to be there, and wasn't sure if the goddess was in attendance or not. Suddenly Athena's face appeared in the altar.

'Goddess, you're here.'

'Yes, I saw you come in. But I was hiding from Luxos. I couldn't let him see me, of course.'

'Of course,' agreed Bremusa. 'For a mortal to see a goddess directly is terrible impiety.'

'I was thinking more of the tedium I might suffer if he started reciting his poetry. But yes, it's impiety too. I'd have been obliged to turn him into a tree or something. So, tell me what's happening. Did Metris help you find Laet?'

Bremusa looked disgusted. 'Metris couldn't find the sea if you took her to the beach. She lied about having powers.'

'Really? Can't she dispel Laet's negative influence?'

'She can't do anything except make daisies and buttercups. I've never encountered a more useless nymph.'

Unexpectedly, the goddess smiled. 'I presume she's the one with whom Luxos has fallen in love?'

'Apparently. Isn't Athens meant to be full of intellectual giants and great artists? How come I keep tripping over this ridiculous young poet?'

'Have you heard any of his poetry?'

'No. Metris likes it so must be bad.'

The shrine was so small that Bremusa's sword touched the wall, making a small metallic sound.

'However, finding Laet is not really such a problem, Goddess. Just go where everyone is making bad decisions. You should have heard the arguments in the agora after she walked through this afternoon. Everyone was buying useless junk and then trying to get their money back, the place was in chaos. The woman's a plague. She'll ruin the peace conference for sure. I don't know how I'm going to thwart her. Do you have any suggestions?'

The Goddess Athena admitted that she didn't. 'Perhaps I'll find some inspiration soon. Meanwhile, try not to let Laet destroy the city. And protect Aristophanes.'

Bremusa was startled. 'Aristophanes? Why?'

'Reports reach me from other worshippers that his play about peace might be influential in making up people's minds.'

Bremusa nodded. 'I see. There might be something in that. I have heard people talking about the play.' She shook her head. 'I hate the theatre. Particularly these ridiculous Athenian comedies.'

'It's good to laugh on occasion, Bremusa.'

'Athenian comedies aren't very respectful to the gods.'

'It's the Dionysia. They have licence to make fun of us.'

'I don't like it.'

'Well, blame Dionysos. What else are you upset about?'

'Nothing.'

'Yes you are. I can tell. I can see that little frown line between your eyebrows.'

Bremusa tried to smooth her forehead, but realised she couldn't fool the goddess about her moods.

'I met Idomeneus,' she muttered.

'Idomeneus? Not Idomeneus of Crete? Isn't he the one—'

Bremusa the Amazon nodded. Much as she hated to admit it,

Idomeneus was the one who would have killed her if Athena hadn't intervened, all those centuries ago.

'How can he possibly still be alive?'

'He's employed as Laet's bodyguard, so it must be her doing. She's kept him alive for centuries. I didn't realise she was so powerful.'

'Neither did I,' admitted Athena. 'I'd no idea Idomeneus was still around. The glory of Crete has long since faded. I don't want you to fight him, Bremusa.'

'We already fought. He attacked me. Laet stopped it because she was bored and had a headache. We'll meet again, I expect.'

'You're not to let your desire for revenge interfere with your mission,' said the goddess.

Bremusa, not willing to argue with Athena but knowing quite well that she wasn't going to back down from a fight with Idomeneus, remained silent.

Luxos

Luxos, bursting out of the shrine, ran right into Metris. He immediately embraced her, taking her slender body in his arms and hugging her tightly. Luxos, while slightly built and undernourished, was not quite as weak as he appeared. Much as he'd disliked it at the time, he had undergone military training with the rest of the Athenian youths. The effects of that had not yet worn off.

'I was just praying I'd meet you again! Athena really worked quickly on this one! She's such a great goddess!'

The nymph smiled. It was a warm night. A slight breeze made her short white dress flutter. There were silver threads in it that seemed to glow faintly, even in the moonlight.

'I've been thinking about you, too. There must be some way of making Athens listen to your poetry. Isn't the city full of wise people? Who's the wisest?'

'Socrates, I suppose.'

Metris took Luxos's hand. 'Then let's go and talk to him.'

They walked off together, heading north into the dark streets of night-time Athens, where there were few lamps lit, oil being so expensive these days, and in short supply. A little later Bremusa emerged from the shrine. Finding no one there, she cursed in a language that was no longer spoken in the world.

'Has that idiot Metris wandered off again? Does she have no concept of actually doing what she's supposed to?'

Aristophanes

Aristophanes knew he'd been neglecting himself. He often did when he was putting on a play. He regretted it. It was the duty of every Athenian of fighting age to keep himself in reasonable shape. In those days the call to arms was never far away, and an unfit citizen was no use on the battlefield. Even if the march outside the city walls didn't end in battle, as was sometimes the case, it was a miserable experience to be trudging along behind your fellow hoplites if you were badly out of condition. The spear, shield and armour of the Athenian warrior could be a weighty burden.

He'd have liked to visit the gymnasium. It would strengthen him and might even clear his mind. Unfortunately he just didn't have the time. There were too many things wrong with his comedy. Shabby props and costumes weren't his only problems. The chorus were singing poorly and urgently needed a better vocal coach. The musicians weren't playing well, the choreography was lacking and the funny dances were less than amusing. As for the precise positioning of the actors on stage during each scene, they'd hardly got started. In the great Theatre of Dionysus Eleuthereus, the audience sat in a huge semicircle around the stage. It was vital that the actors worked together, moving correctly into position and standing in the right place at all times. Otherwise the drama would suffer and the jokes wouldn't work. They'd now fallen so far behind with this that Aristophanes had been forced to call extra rehearsals, which hadn't gone down that well with the cast.

'It's lucky I've written such a good script,' he mused, as he walked through the pale light of dawn towards the rehearsal space. Or I'd lose all hope.

Aristophanes was seriously worried that they might not even make it to performance. Cancelling the play would be humiliating in the extreme, and could make it difficult for him to find a producer next year. Even so, it might be preferable to taking the shambles they had at the moment on stage. If he did, the Athenians would certainly laugh, but not in a good way.

Aristophanes kicked several stones as he walked. Recently he'd been feeling vaguely angry about everything, and particularly angry about his rivals Eupolis and Leucon. There was no denying it, he loathed them. He really couldn't stand the thought of either of them winning first prize. He idly brushed his hand over the Herm at the corner of the street – Aristophanes had always liked these little statues on the corners of Athens, with their cheery faces and confident upright penises – and almost bumped into Socrates, coming briskly in the opposite direction. The morning air was chilly but the philosopher was dressed, as always, in a plain chiton, and hadn't bothered to cover it with a cloak. Socrates never wore a cloak. He seemed immune to bad weather.

They greeted each other politely.

'Good morning, Socrates. Off to the gymnasium for some exercise before a hard day's philosophy?'

'I am. And you?'

'I've no time to exercise. I'm busy with rehearsals.'

'Ah . . . Any jokes about me in your play this year?

'Why do you say that?'

Socrates laughed. 'Because you always make jokes about me.'

'And I always admire how well you take them!'

It was true. Socrates did take it well, unlike the Athenian politicians. They might make a show of approving the way comic playwrights ridiculed them, because it demonstrated what a fine, free democracy the city was. In reality, they seethed in private, and sometimes sought revenge.

'Socrates, are you going to Callias's symposium tonight?'

'I wasn't planning to. Isn't it meant to be for playwrights and actors?'

'Mainly. But if I have to listen to Eupolis and Leucon droning on about how well their rehearsals are going I might do something I'll regret. There will be others there too, you could come along. Callias likes to pretend he understands philosophy, Zeus knows why.'

'How would my presence help?'

'Just say something clever if you see me reaching for my weapon.' Aristophanes chuckled. '"Reaching for my weapon". Rather a good line. Must remember it. Audiences always love a good double entendre.'

Socrates laughed too. In the past, he'd appreciated Aristophanes' clever wordplay. 'Like when your actor playing Euripides was hunting for an argument in his bag, saying he was going to pull out something "strong and meaty"?'

'That was a good one! The audience roared.'

'They did. Though the real Euripides looked rather grim, as I remember.'

'Well, he has a poor sense of humour. Just look at his plays.'

Aristophanes walked on. The streets were still quiet. The morning bustle would start soon, though the morning bustle in Athens was not what it had been. There used to be a scramble for the best places in the agora. Merchants and their servants could be seen at all hours, vying for the best spot. That didn't happen now. There weren't enough goods to sell.

Round the next corner Aristophanes ran into Hyperbolus. He tried to ignore him but Hyperbolus stood in his way. He was a large man, strong, and heavily bearded.

'Hyperbolus? What are you doing here? Shouldn't you be practising your shouting?'

Hyperbolus glared at him. 'Aristophanes, you make me sick. You and your rich friends. You can't stand it that an ordinary man like me has some influence in this city. You'd like to go back to the time when rich people ran everything.'

'I'd like to go back to a time when Athens wasn't run by self-serving buffoons.'

Even when he wasn't addressing the assembly, Hyperbolus had a very loud voice. It boomed out over the quiet streets. 'If you keep insulting the city that way, you're going to be in trouble.'

'For such a determined democrat, Hyperbolus, you're not very keen on considering other people's views.'

'Not if their views are traitorous.'

'Hoping for an end to the war isn't traitorous.'

'It is if it means giving in to these filthy Spartans.'

By now they were almost nose to nose. Hyperbolus was a far larger man but Aristophanes didn't intend to back down.

'I've fought for Athens more times than you have, Hyperbolus. But it's time to end this war. You and General Lamachus like conflict. It's good for your careers. Everyone else is sick of it.'

'Everyone else is sick of you, you and your vile, unpatriotic, insulting plays. I'm warning you, Aristophanes, if you keep harping on about peace there's going to be trouble. What's your new play called?'

'*Peace*.'

'Then I predict trouble.'

Socrates

Socrates usually exercised in the morning. At forty-nine, he was still a strong man. He'd grown up as a stonemason, helping his father hew rocks, and since then he'd never neglected his health. He left the Lyceum with friends, Menexenus and others. Not teaching, though talking, as always, of philosophy.

'I just don't understand this,' said young Menexenus. 'You say knowledge is contained inside people? And learning is merely a process of remembering? I can't see that at all.'

Socrates nodded as they passed beyond the boundary of the Lyceum. He was fond of young Menexenus, an Athenian of good character. They paused under the three olive trees, a familiar landmark.

'I could demonstrate my meaning, if someone with little knowledge appeared,' said Socrates.

Abruptly there was a dull thud, followed by a cry of pain. The philosopher and his followers looked round to see a figure sprawled in the dirt, comically spreadeagled, face down.

'It's young Luxos,' said Menexenus. 'He's fallen over that small twig.'

'Perfect,' said Socrates. 'Luxos, would you care to help me with a demonstration?'

A young woman in an unusually short dress was bending over Luxos, soothing his hurt and helping him to his feet. The young poet clambered upright, embarrassed at his display of clumsiness so close to the training grounds. Luxos generally avoided the city's gymnasiums, not being very good at any sort of physical activity.

'Not right now, Socrates,' he said. 'We've come to you for advice.'

There was a general lack of interest in this from the group, though Socrates paid polite attention.

'We thought you might be able to help,' said the girl, and smiled.

Socrates nodded. 'Does Luxos want to know how to get his poetry heard by the Greek masses?'

'Oh,' said the girl, and looked impressed. 'You really are wise.'

'The subject has come up before.' Socrates smiled.

Nearby there was the sound of discuses landing, thrown by athletes in the Lyceum. Metris, rather cleverly, had by now manoeuvred them a few paces back from Socrates' companions, where they could talk without being overheard.

'I don't think I can help you,' said Socrates. 'I would if I could, but I can't see any way for you to attract a rich sponsor.'

'Are you going to Callias's symposium tonight?' asked Luxos.

'I am ... rather unwillingly ...'

'Could you get me in?'

Socrates pursed his lips. 'Callias is not that enlightened when it comes to inviting penniless poets to his drinking parties.'

Luxos was immediately disheartened. 'It's so unfair.'

The philosopher turned to Metris. He noticed the small flute she wore on a string around her neck.

'Can you play that flute well?'

'I can.'

Socrates lowered his voice to a whisper. 'Well, you could sneak in the servants' door at the back and pretend to be the entertainment.'

Luxos's face lit up. 'That's a brilliant idea! Once I'm in there I'm bound to get a chance to recite some poetry. I'll get a sponsor in no time. Thanks, Socrates!'

Socrates nodded. 'Don't tell anyone I suggested it,' he whispered, then went on his way.

Hyperbolus

Hyperbolus, as a strong supporter of Athens' democratic faction, could not enter the Pegasus barber shop, where Euphranor the weapon-maker conducted most of his business. Similarly, Euphranor, a conservative, would not have been welcomed in the back room of the tavern on the edge of Piraeus where the important democrats met to discuss their affairs. So they met on top of the acropolis, outside the Parthenon, where anyone might be. For a place to hide in plain sight, it was ideal. The Parthenon was renowned as one of the finest buildings in the world. Everyone met there at some time, even political enemies. There was nothing suspicious about them exchanging a few words.

Neither liked the other. In past times, Hyperbolus had castigated Euphranor in front of the whole assembly, accusing him of exploiting the workers who toiled in his armoury, and using his wealth to bribe politicians. For his part, Euphranor had bribed politicians to lay into Hyperbolus, blackening his name, spreading rumours about him and paying people to vote against him. Now they were allies, supporting the same cause. They both wanted the war to continue. It suited them to put aside their differences for a while.

'I don't like the way things are going,' said Hyperbolus. 'It was a step forward when the peace conference broke up, but there's still a lot of pressure to end the war. I particularly don't like the way everyone is talking about Aristophanes' play. You know it's called *Peace*?'

'It's just a play,' said Euphranor. 'Is it that important?'

'Who knows? It might be the thing that tips the balance.'

'Antimachus is his choregos. He assured us he'd sabotage it. He hasn't been giving Aristophanes any money.'

Hyperbolus frowned. 'I know. But Aristophanes isn't giving up. What if he gets funds from somewhere else?'

'I don't suppose there's much we can do about it. The plays at the Dionysia are sacred, even Aristophanes' obscene comedies. We can't be seen to be interfering with it. We'll just have to trust Antimachus to ruin it.'

'I suppose so.' Hyperbolus would like to have taken stronger action, but he knew Euphranor was right. The Dionysia was sacred. It wouldn't do to be caught interfering with it. Charges of impiety could follow. Athens was full of informers. You never quite knew who you could trust. They walked on under the gaze of Hephaistos and Hera, god and goddess, carved on the east pediment of the great temple. There they stood for a moment, discussing other matters, but fell silent as an unfamiliar woman walked by. Tall and dark. Beautiful, though strangely dressed. Certainly not a native of the city. Moments after she'd gone, Hyperbolus turned to Euphranor.

'You know, why take chances? Why don't we just kill Aristophanes and get it over with?'

Euphranor's eyes opened wide. 'Kill Aristophanes? That's a brilliant idea. Why didn't we think of it before?'

'We could hire someone to do it tonight.'

On the steps of the Parthenon, Laet halted and looked back at the two plotting politicians. She smiled to herself.

It never takes much.

She went inside the temple to look at the frieze which, she had heard, was one of the finest works of art in the city.

Luxos

Luxos and Metris watched as two slaves carrying amphoras of wine entered Callias's house via the alleyway at the back.

'I've never seen such a big house,' said Metris.

'Richest man in Athens, so they say.'

Another wagon-load of supplies trundled past. Seeing the size of the house, the stream of luxury goods being carried inside, and the number of slaves and servants in attendance, Luxos and Metris took a step back, temporarily intimidated.

'Don't worry,' said Luxos.

Wisdom outweighs any wealth – Sophocles

'We can outwit them.' He marched confidently along the alley, his lyre in his hand. 'The party will be full of influential people and I'm going to give them some poetry they'll never forget.'

The door at the back was opened by a servant, a woman well-versed in keeping out freeloaders. Her face set grimly at the sight of Luxos and Metris, as likely a pair of freeloaders as she'd seen for some time.

'What do you want?'

'Flute player, dancer and poet reporting for duty,' announced Luxos. 'Part of tonight's entertainment.'

The servant eyed Metris. With her pretty face and a flute round her neck, she could be a hired musician. As for Luxos, she wasn't convinced.

'You're a dancer?'

'Yes. And a talented poet to boot.'

'Poets,' grunted the servant, in a tone which suggested she wasn't a devotee. 'The house is already full of them.'

'Old-fashioned, past their prime, no doubt. I'm here as part of the new generation.'

'And to fill yourself up with as much food as your stomach will hold, I expect,' said the servant, shrewdly. She was on the point of refusing them entry when she noticed Metris smiling at her. There was something about the nymph's smile that was hard to resist. It felt as if she was transferring some primal form of happiness.

'Fine. Come in. Entertain the crowd. But keep out of our way in the kitchens.'

Laet

At the edge of the agora, Laet pointed out the Altar of Pity. 'Rather an important shrine.'

Idomeneus was unimpressed. 'It looks like a useless old piece of rock. Why is it important?'

Laet stood beside the ancient altar, examining it carefully. It was worn down, so eroded with age as to be almost featureless. 'It's the place of last resort. Athenians come here when everything else has failed. When you've been to all the temples, and asked every god for help, and your hope has gone, you can come here. There's no special prayer to say. No particular offering has to be made. You just ask for pity.'

She placed her hand above the small altar. 'Can you feel it?'

'Feel what?'

'All the desperate pleas of Athenians down the ages.'

Idomeneus couldn't feel anything. He remained silent. Laet's eyes glinted. She laid her hand on the altar. There was a sharp crack as it split in two and fell in the dust. Without another word, she walked away. Idomeneus hurried after her.

'Did you just destroy the Athenians' last hope?' he asked, catching up with her.

'I believe so.'

'Isn't that more than Kleonike asked you to do?'

'Probably. It's never really wise to engage my services. If people are foolish enough to do so, they must live with the consequences. I do like to do a very thorough job. Which reminds me – Aristophanes now has a price on his head, if you're interested.'

Aristophanes

At Callias's house there is much pleasure
For he has crabs for dinner, rays besides,
and hares, and women with light twinkling feet

Eupolis, *The Flatterers*

There were torches on the porch, illuminating the entrance to Callias's house, and rows of oil lamps inside. Few people could afford to burn so much lamp oil these days; Callias was not averse to displaying his wealth. Aristophanes trudged inside in the wake of Eupolis and Leucon, whom he'd met in the street outside. He'd managed to remain civil, though if it had been a longer street, he'd probably have started an argument.

Callias greeted them in the hallway. He was a stout man, though not outrageously so, given his enormous fortune and healthy appetite. His parents and grandparents were important Athenians, statesmen with rich connections to the silver mines. Callias wasn't a statesman, or even a renowned man of business. He was mainly known for spending money.

Though he does still have some aspirations to be regarded as a thinker, reflected Aristophanes, noticing the statue of Solon the Wise in the hallway. I've seen him hanging round Socrates, pretending he knows what the philosopher is talking about.

'Eupolis! Leucon! Aristophanes! Our three comic geniuses! You honour me by coming to my house. I do hope none of you are going to satirise me this year!'

Aristophanes imagined he'd like nothing better than to be lambasted from the stage. It was a sort of fame; even a mark of honour. At least it meant you were important enough to be talked about. Politicians didn't enjoy it, but a man like Callias would take it in good part. Cleisthenes, a well-known Athenian with many theatrical connections, always laughed uproariously when Aristophanes mocked his effeminacy.

Callias led them through into his main dining room, which was vast, and illuminated by more oil lamps than any of the diners had ever seen lit at one time in a private dwelling.

'I know you'll have us all laughing after we've eaten!'

Eupolis and Leucon laughed easily in Callias's company. That was the right thing to do. There was no sense in not laughing with the rich man when you were in his house, eating his food. Unfortunately for Aristophanes, he was in too poor a temper to join in.

'Are they serving wine yet?' he asked, but no one heard him. Callias was spluttering at some joke from Eupolis. Eupolis was young, like Aristophanes. He'd started in the theatre early, like Aristophanes. They had a lot in common. Aristophanes was disliking him more every minute.

There were over a dozen couches in the dining room. Callias's symposium was on a larger scale than most. Some of the guests who'd arrived early were reclining together on the couches, some were still standing. Socrates was there, in the corner, sitting quietly. Servants were bringing in platters of food, meat and fish, and Callias was bragging about how he'd personally visited the market that day, to make sure only the best produce was used.

'I've hired the finest cook in Athens! You won't believe what he does with pastry. Eupolis, I met Simonides at the market, he's your producer this year, isn't he? He was buying a huge amount of paint from that new Theban stallholder, was that for your scenery?'

'Yes, we've got a lot of expensive decoration going on,' replied Eupolis. 'I had to hire three new painters this week.'

'Is there a wine shortage?' demanded Aristophanes. 'Some people could really use a drink.'

No one heard him. He decided to take matters into his own hands. It was polite to wait till everyone arrived, and the correct ceremonies had been conducted, before you started drinking, but

Aristophanes wasn't in the mood for ceremony. He cursed Callias under his breath as he headed for the kitchen.

What sort of fool invites playwrights to their house and doesn't give them wine as soon as they arrive?

As Aristophanes entered the kitchen there was a commotion going on. The newly hired chef was shouting at someone. Chefs were notoriously temperamental.

'You young ruffians. Have you been stealing my food?'

Aristophanes looked beyond the chef to where two young figures were looking rather guilty: Luxos and a young woman he'd never seen before. Pretty girl, he noticed, though rather embarrassed at the moment, probably because of the loaf of bread poorly concealed about her person.

'Luxos! What are you doing here?'

'I'm part of the entertainment!' said Luxos.

'Entertainment?' cried the chef. 'They've been stealing from the kitchen! I'm going to have them arrested.'

Aristophanes shook his head. Luxos was annoying, of course, and apparently not above pilfering food, but he didn't want to see him locked up. If nothing else, he'd done good work on the spying mission. And he was a fellow member of the Pandionis tribe, unfortunately.

'It's all right. The eh ... entertainers ... are entitled to a meal. I'm sure Callias said it was fine.'

'Well, get them out of my kitchen,' roared the chef. 'I've got enough to do without looking out for thieving flute players and hungry poets.'

Luxos and the girl wasted no time in fleeing the kitchen. Aristophanes pursued them into the hallway.

'What's the idea of forcing your way into this house?'

'We're the entertainment,' said Luxos.

'No you're not! Depart immediately or people will think I invited you. They know we're in the same tribe.'

With the kitchen now hostile territory, thanks to the imbecilic

Luxos, Aristophanes was forced to return to the dining room, still without a goblet of wine. He cursed under his breath. He should have known to fortify himself before setting out.

General Lamachus and the statesman Nicias were reclining on adjacent couches. Nicias looked far older than the general, though the age difference could only have been seven or eight years. The general was a tough, grizzled man who led by example on the battlefield, and showed no sign of his powers diminishing with the passing years. Lamachus had his opponents, and Aristophanes didn't like him, but no one could ever accuse him of hanging back when there was fighting to be done, or sending others to die in his place. He leaned over to speak to Nicias.

'I hear you couldn't get the Spartans back to the negotiating table.'

'I couldn't get anyone back to the negotiating table. The Athenians are acting just as badly as the Spartans.'

'I wouldn't say we were acting badly. We're simply not ready for peace. What's wrong with that?'

'What is wrong is that it will destroy the city.'

'Really? I'd say we've had the upper hand in the fighting recently.'

'Recently?' said Nicias. 'Perhaps. But it wasn't long ago that the war was going badly. Then we'd have been pleased with an honourable peace. But as soon as things improve a little, Athens starts thinking maybe we can win the war.'

Aristophanes nodded absently. What Nicias said was true. The phenomenon had been commented on widely enough. When the Athenians gained an advantage, they didn't want peace. They wanted to press on with the war. Soon enough, the Spartans would gain the advantage. That made the Athenians think that peace might not be such a bad idea, but by then, the Spartans were no longer willing to negotiate. The cycle kept repeating, as it had for the past decade.

'If we don't make peace now, we'll both be destroyed,' said

Nicias. Aristophanes didn't hear the general's reply, being diverted by the sight of Leucon and Eupolis sharing a couch. For rival playwrights, they made a show of getting along well. When the titles of the comedies in this year's Dionysia had been announced – *Peace* by Aristophanes, *The Flatterers* by Eupolis, and *The Clansmen* by Leucon – his two competitors had made a great show of wishing each other luck. Aristophanes loathed all his rivals so comprehensively that he could hardly imagine wishing any of them luck. Callias bustled over and motioned for him to take the next empty couch.

'I'm sure you three comedy writers have a lot to talk about! I'm hoping Euripides will be here soon, you know he's presenting a tragedy this year.'

Euripides was a famous, if controversial, figure. Neither Eupolis nor Leucon seemed impressed by the prospect of his attendance.

'I don't set a lot of store by today's tragedies,' said Leucon.

'Neither do I,' agreed Eupolis. 'The standard has gone down dreadfully in the past few years. I've always thought that comedy is much harder to do.'

'I do agree! The common citizen doesn't realise how hard it is to make people laugh.'

Aristophanes gritted his teeth. He was starting to think the wine was never going to arrive. He ignored the couch next to the playwrights and joined Socrates on his.

'I hate these theatrical types.'

'That must make your life awkward,' said Socrates.

'Has Callias got something against drinking?'

'I don't think so. Why?'

'He hasn't served any wine yet. I'd have thought you'd have noticed that, being such a famous intellectual. What's the delay? The man owns his own vineyard, dammit.'

'He's probably just waiting for our garlands; look, here they are now.'

Four young men appeared in the room with garlands of flowers for each guest to wear. They were pleasant garlands, fresh and colourful. As the guests put them on their heads there was general appreciation shown towards their host. Callias beamed.

'And now it's time choose our symposiarch.'

The symposiarch acted as toastmaster for the evening, and decided how strongly the wine should be mixed.

'I'll do it,' said Aristophanes, immediately.

Callias looked at him, and then round at the others.

'Any other volunteers?'

'I said I'll do it!' Aristophanes turned to the nearest servant. 'Bring the wine and make it strong!'

Bremusa

The moon was obscured by clouds and the night-time streets were very dark. Even with her superior night-vision, Bremusa couldn't see far in front of her. She wondered where Metris had got to.

Probably still hanging around with that moronic young poet. I never thought much of nymphs and this has confirmed my opinion. If the Goddess Athena sends you on an important mission and the first thing you do is become infatuated with a juvenile poet with too much hair and a poor work ethic, what does that say about your character? Not much. But nymphs are like that. No sense at all.

She halted, peering around her, trying to get her bearings. What was she doing here anyway?

I don't know how to defeat Laet. If Athena had allowed me to kill her, I might have had a chance of succeeding. Now it's hopeless. I have no clever plan. I've never had a clever plan.

The depression that had been gnawing at Bremusa since she

arrived in Athens began to grow. She felt like a stupid, ancient, uneducated woman, a relic from the past, blundering around in a city she didn't understand, surrounded by poets, artists and philosophers with whom she had nothing in common. Now she was meant to protect Aristophanes, another task she didn't relish.

I loathe the theatre. I don't understand why people want to sit and watch people pretending to be other people. What's the point? I was born underneath a horse, on the way to battle. We didn't have theatres.

The Amazon bumped into a statue of a naked man throwing a discus. She glared at it.

I don't like their statues either. Or their paintings. The whole city is degenerate. I wouldn't care if Sparta destroyed it.

She scowled. 'Wait till I get my hands on Idomeneus. I'd have beaten him at Troy if my foot hadn't slipped. I'll make him sorry. And Metris too. What's the matter with her? If my mother had caught me hanging round a young poet when I was her age, she'd have chopped my head off.'

Bremusa carried on, her mood worsening all the time.

Aristophanes

Callias may be a fool, an easy target for flatterers and fortune hunters, who will probably divest him of his fortune one day. And he may be too keen to welcome inferior dramatists into his house. But I will give him credit for one thing. When he finally gets round to serving the wine, it's good quality, and there's an endless supply. Aristophanes was enjoying the role of symposiarch. The huge krater of wine in the centre of the room was emptying rapidly as each guest's cup was filled again and again. Aristophanes called for the krater to be refilled, meanwhile ignoring all requests for the wine to be diluted, or handed round more slowly.

'Stop complaining, you pathetic little weeds, and drink some wine. I've written better plays than all of you, I've fought better on the battlefield, and I've slept with more hetaerae than you. Now I'm going to show you how an Athenian can drink.'

It was not the sort of challenge his companions could ignore. After an hour or so of heavy drinking, the room was in uproar, and Aristophanes was feeling a lot better about life. He flung his arm round Socrates' shoulder.

'You're not a bad chap, Socrates. Much too keen on lecturing people about philosophy, but you did fight well at Delium, and you can drink a reasonable-sized cup of wine. Talking of which, why are our goblets empty? Bring more wine! Stronger this time!'

'Is that really a good idea?' said Socrates.

'Who's symposiarch, you or me? Bring more wine!'

Aristophanes laughed as the aged Leucon, so-called comic poet, fell off his couch.

'Ha. Can't take his wine like us, Socrates. We're old soldiers. We're tough!'

Aristophanes noticed Callias was looking a little displeased. He had no idea why.

'Perhaps it's time for a pause in the proceedings,' said their host. 'I think it's time for some entertainment.'

One end of the room had been cleared, to act as a stage. There was a fancy embroidered curtain as a backdrop, and from behind it stepped a surprisingly beautiful young woman. She carried a flute, and smiled cheerfully as she emerged.

Callias looked puzzled. 'I don't remember hiring her. Where's my secretary?'

The secretary was lying drunk under a couch, unable to keep up with the company. He wasn't the only one. Aristophanes kept sending the wine round, and several guests were finding it diffi-cult to maintain the pace.

Two actors, newcomers to the party, shouted at Callias.

'Can she play the flute?'

'Let her play anyway! She's beautiful.'

'If you like that sort of thing.'

Metris began to play. Even though many of the guests were by now rather the worse for wear, it was soon obvious that she was a talented performer. Not only that, there was something about her that seemed to radiate good cheer. Aristophanes found himself tapping out the rhythm with his feet. His garland of flowers fell off. He jammed it back on and began to dance.

Idomeneus

Laet had informed Idomeneus that if he wanted to earn some extra money, there was now a price on Aristophanes' head. Euphranor was offering a reward. She didn't say how she'd learned this, but Idomeneus assumed she'd something to do with initiating it. He accepted the offer. He'd never been poor since travelling with Laet, but he wasn't wealthy either. He used to be, centuries ago, and he still remembered that.

Before they parted he asked Laet if she needed anything. She shook her head. She rarely needed much. She wasn't that demanding a woman. She ate little, quickly became bored by luxuries, and apparently had no sexual desire. She often preferred to remain silent for long periods. Despite their long association, Idomeneus didn't really know what motivated her. He knew she liked to ruin other people's lives. She'd been doing that for eight hundred years, but she'd never offered him any sort of explanation. Perhaps the semi-divines didn't need the same sort of motivations that humans did.

For most of that time, Idomeneus of Crete had been her bodyguard. Or servant, perhaps, though that's not how he liked to think of himself. He'd been a military leader, back in his natural life span. He didn't serve anyone. But when a man had his life extended by such an amount, he was prepared to do a few things he'd rather not do.

Last week Idomeneus had killed two men who'd tried to waylay them on their way to Athens. He ran each of them through in an instant. He'd never lost his fighting skill. Afterwards he couldn't understand why the robbers had thought they could attack them.

Why did they think they could rob me? I wouldn't say I looked like an easy target. Perhaps they were driven on by Laet's beauty. Maybe they thought they could take her as a prize. Fools.

Or perhaps Laet made them do it. When she extended her powers, people did act in ridiculous ways. It might have been her idea of a treat for her bodyguard. She knew he liked to see action every now and then.

Idomeneus had learned that Aristophanes had been invited to a symposium at Callias's house. He took directions and made his way there, though progress was slow. The night was dark and he had to conceal himself several times from the groups of Scythian archers who policed the streets at night. As an alien in the city, he knew they'd be suspicious of him, large and heavily armed. He finally made it to the street with the statue of Apollo holding a flute. He knew he was close to Callias's mansion and settled down to wait. At some point Aristophanes was going to emerge, and Idomeneus was going to kill him.

Aristophanes

When the girl finished playing her flute there was a lot of applause, and a lot of laughter at those individuals who, moved to dance but too intoxicated to keep up, had collapsed on their couches, or underneath them. Aristophanes' mood had transformed. Why was he worrying? He was the best comic dramatist in Athens. He was the best poet. He wrote the funniest scenes. Was anyone going to defeat him in a contest? Let them try.

'I can beat any man here at cottabus!' yelled Eupolis.

Aristophanes wasn't going to decline a challenge like that. 'I'll take you on!' he roared.

Cottabus was a popular after-dinner game. Players had to fling the dregs of their wine at a small statue, attempting to knock it from its perch so it fell into a saucer below. They did this while reclining on their couches. After an evening of drinking, it could be a challenging task. On Callias's orders servants bustled in, setting up the stand with the tiny statue on top.

'Watch this!' cried Aristophanes, in the general direction of Socrates. 'It takes a fine eye and a steady hand to win at cottabus. If you're a dramatist of unusual skill, that helps too.'

Aristophanes made short work of Eupolis, knocking the statue from its perch with deadly aim while his opponent flailed around hopelessly.

'Much as he does in the theatre!' yelled Aristophanes, very amused. Nicias was too statesmanlike to play, but General Lamachus was always up for a challenge. He put up more of a fight but Aristophanes saw him off too, before scoring another fine triumph over some young man he hadn't been introduced to, a lover of Callias's, possibly. He was a good-looking youth. *Far too good-looking for Callias,* thought Aristophanes, *but when you were as rich as he was, you could buy all the handsome lovers you wanted.*

Aristophanes was looking round for more opponents when he was interrupted by a voice he'd rather not have heard.

'And now, our special entertainment of the evening – lyric poetry from Athens' favourite up-and-coming young poet, Luxos!'

Luxos, having introduced himself, appeared on the small stage, holding his cheap lyre.

'I know I didn't invite him,' said Callias. 'Aristophanes, is he a friend of yours?'

'I've never seen him before.'

'Throw the scoundrel out!' cried Eupolis. But Callias, full of wine and keen to recline after dancing far too vigorously for a man of his age and bulk, didn't seem to mind.

'Oh, let him recite, I need a rest anyway.'

Luxos's youthful face lit up. Against the odds, he'd succeeded. He was finally going to be able to recite his poetry to an influential audience. Aristophanes chuckled. Luxos was a young scoundrel, but if he was willing to make that much effort, perhaps he deserved his chance. As his female companion looked on, rather adoringly, people noticed, Luxos began to recite:

Immortal meadows of many-coloured flowers
welcome in their embrace—

And at that moment there was an almighty commotion as the door burst open and Alcibiades arrived. Alcibiades, the most famous, most controversial, loudest, wealthiest, wildest young man in Athens, marched into the dining room with a garland of flowers askew on his head, an entourage of young aristocrats and prostitutes in his wake.

'Callias, you dog!' he roared. 'You think you can have a drinking party without Alcibiades? Hand over a cup of wine and let's get this party under way!'

Immediately the room degenerated into chaos as the wealthy youth of Athens took over. Suddenly it was full of dancing girls, dancing boys and roaring young drunks, standing on couches, yelling, laughing and singing. Everyone was swept up into the celebration. Only Socrates held back, remaining in his place on his couch, quietly observing. He noticed Luxos on stage, still holding his lyre. Realising that he could no longer be heard, and no one was paying any attention to him, the young poet looked forlorn. Metris took his hand and they watched the drunken rev-elry for a few minutes before disappearing offstage. Luxos trudged away like a reprimanded schoolboy, his eyes on the ground, his shoulders slumped in misery.

Alcibiades' face, normally handsome, was flushed red from drinking. 'Aristophanes!' he yelled. 'Are you putting me in your play this year? I'll be disappointed if you don't!'

Aristophanes smiled and nodded. He wasn't putting him in his play. When someone was that keen to be mocked on stage, it wasn't that much fun doing it.

'Time for the procession!' yelled one of Alcibiades' friends.

'Everybody outside!' cried Alcibiades.

Aristophanes did enjoy a good after-party procession. Led by Alcibiades and Callias, everyone grabbed hold of torches, filled up their wine cups, slung their cloaks over their shoulders and headed outside to parade through the dark streets; not an uncommon event after a riotous symposium like the one they'd just attended.

Aristophanes was still in a fine mood. Some drinking, some dancing, a few victories at cottabus – life felt much better. Looking at his problems now, they didn't seem too bad.

So, my producer is a miser. Eupolis and Leucon have more money to spend. Do they have my talent? Of course not. Once I've ironed out a few problems with the choreography I'll have a play fit to win any Dionysia.

He marched along with a torch in one hand and a cup of wine in the other, bawling out one of his favourite drinking songs.

That Callias, he's not such a bad soul really. Fat fool, of course, and tardy with the wine, but generous in the end.

When it came to the chorus, Aristophanes noticed that no one was joining in. That was odd. It was a popular song, recounting Athens' great victory at Salamis. He looked around and realised he was on his own. Somehow, in the darkness, he'd wandered away from the procession. He looked at his cup of wine. It was empty. His torch flickered and went out. He felt a chill breeze blowing through his summer cloak. His good mood vanished with the wind. Now he felt drunk, but not pleasantly so. He realised he'd been fooling himself about his play being nearly ready. It wasn't. The play was a shambles. Again he had an alarming vision of being booed off stage by angry Athenians. An overwhelming depression settled in. He felt lonely and far from home. He needed rest. He needed sleep.

He didn't need, or expect, a large man with a bronze breast-plate to appear from nowhere, with a sword in his hand.

'Aristophanes?'

'Who wants to know?'

'Me. I'm here to kill you.'

Bremusa

Bremusa withdrew into the shadows as a noisy torchlight procession approached. A great group of revellers, mainly drunken men, with a few women behind them. She realised they must have come from the symposium at Callias's house and she wondered why Aristophanes wasn't with them. As the procession passed her, a voice from a house nearby shouted for them to be quiet and stop disturbing the peace. The leader of the procession hurled back some cheerful abuse and started up another raucous song. Bremusa remained hidden till they'd gone, then hurried on.

It was worrying that Aristophanes hadn't been with his companions. She sensed that something bad was about to happen and picked up her pace. She ran round another dark corner and suddenly came upon Aristophanes and Idomeneus. Idomeneus had a sword in his hand. Aristophanes was fumbling for something at his belt. Perhaps he thought there was a blade there, though there wasn't. Then he fell over.

So much for Athens' greatest comic playwright, thought Bremusa. *Too drunk to find a weapon or even stay on his feet.*

She sprinted forward, unsheathing her sword.

'Step back, Idomeneus.'

Idomeneus whirled round. When he saw Bremusa approaching he didn't waste time in speech, he just flew at her with his sword raised. They engaged immediately and there was furious combat on the dark muddy street, the only illumination coming from an oil lamp which burned dimly in front of a small shrine nearby. Their swords clashed noisily and rapidly. Idomeneus of Crete was a very strong man, and a skilful fighter. He'd killed many enemies before the Trojan walls. He'd killed Amazons too. The memory of this infuriated Bremusa, and it was not just her own defeat for which she sought revenge. They fought a desperate battle in the dim light, till it happened that their swords clashed in such a way as to make them both take a step back.

Idomeneus glared at the Amazon. 'Athena's not here to help you now.'

'And Laet's not here to help you.'

They re-engaged, even more furiously. Bremusa matched him in skill but his strength began to drive her back. His blade slid over hers and she felt a sharp pain as it cut her shoulder. Completely enraged, Bremusa yelled out the battle cry of the Amazons and flung herself forward like one of the Furies, determined to kill him. So violent was her assault that she succeeded in driving him back. She wounded him too, a cut to the left arm that made him wince, though it didn't slow him.

'Die, you Amazon bitch,' yelled Idomeneus, and advanced again, his sword flashing towards her. Bremusa blocked desperately as she was driven back. Idomeneus's strength was beginning to tell. At that moment they were interrupted by the sound of whistles and pounding feet, very close.

Idomeneus paused, though he maintained his guard.

'Scythian archers,' he muttered. There was a second's indecision, then he took off, disappearing into the darkness. Bremusa whirled round. Aristophanes was sitting on the ground. She dragged him to his feet.

'Quickly, unless you want to get arrested.'

She dragged him past the shrine and through several small vegetable gardens, escaping the street before the Scythian archers arrived. Aristophanes was too intoxicated to move quickly, but didn't protest as she shepherded him to safety. When they'd gone far enough to avoid detection, they halted.

'Where do you live?'

'I can't remember,' mumbled Aristophanes. There was a pause. 'Take me to Theodota's.'

'Theodota? The hetaera? Won't she have another client at this time?'

To Bremusa's annoyance, Aristophanes sat down. He was still drunk, and now he looked depressed as well.

'I don't want to go home alone,' he said. 'Do you live somewhere?'

'Yes, but you can't go there. Tell me where you live!'

'I can't remember.'

Bremusa could hear voices, not far off. She wasn't sure if the Scythian archers had given up looking for them or not. They might arrive at any moment. The Amazon didn't know if arrest would have serious consequences for Aristophanes, but she couldn't allow herself to be apprehended for causing a disturbance in the street. The Goddess Athena would be annoyed if she were careless enough to get arrested while on a mission for her.

'Damn it,' she muttered. She helped Aristophanes to his feet, put her arm round his shoulder to support him, then set off towards the tavern where she'd rented a room. She gritted her teeth as the wound in her shoulder began to sting.

'Slow down,' said Aristophanes, slurring his words.

'We can't slow down. Do you have to drink so much?'

Around Callias's mansion the streets were beautifully tended. In the area where Bremusa had rented a room, they weren't. They were cracked, muddy and treacherous. It made walking at night difficult, and potentially messy too, if you came across one of the open sewers. It took quite a long time to drag the intoxicated Aristophanes to the tavern. Bremusa's mood, already bad, had worsened.

I don't want to be looking after this fool. I want to hunt for Idomeneus.

Bremusa was heartened that she'd managed to wound him. She was aware, however, that as the fight progressed, he'd been driving her back. Though their fighting skill was equal, his strength gave him an advantage that she'd not been able to overcome. Despite this, she refused to contemplate defeat. *I'll still kill him next time we meet.*

At least there was no one awake at the tavern to see her hauling Aristophanes up the stairs. Inside her tiny room there was a small bed and nothing else. She let Aristophanes go and he fell face down on the bed.

'Thanks for the rescue, strange barbarian woman.'

Bremusa did not regard herself as a barbarian, though that was undoubtedly how those around her in the city would see her. Anyone who wasn't a native Greek speaker was a barbarian. Zeus alone knew what they thought of her in the tavern, with her armour and sword, and her heavy accent. She looked at Aristophanes, drunk on the bed.

'At Delphi there's an inscription. "Nothing in excess". You could learn from that.'

'I will reward your assistance with free theatre tickets,' mumbled the playwright.

'Don't bother.'

Aristophanes fell asleep. Bremusa stared at him with some dislike. Then she spread her cloak on the floor, made a pillow from her tunic, and lay down to sleep.

Luxos

Luxos arrived home, very depressed. 'I was so close to having my poetry heard! A plague on Alcibiades and his aristocratic drunken revelry.'

He sat down heavily on one of the two rickety wooden chairs in his single room. 'I'm going to complain to Aristophanes.'

Metris looked dubious. 'That might not be the best idea. I think he was annoyed because everyone thought he invited you to the symposium.'

'How do you know that?' asked Luxos.

'I heard him say "Now everyone thinks I invited that idiot Luxos to the symposium".'

'Oh.'

'At least we got food,' said Metris brightly, emptying the bag of supplies they'd filched from the party.

Luxos slumped in his chair. It had been a relief to eat, after a long period of hunger, but that pleasure had now worn off. 'Maybe everyone's right. Maybe I don't deserve to be a poet. No one's ever going to listen to me.'

'Could you put on your own play?'

Luxos shook his head. He was normally an optimistic youth but his optimism had been crushed by the evening's events, and by the pervasive cloud of unhappiness that now lay over Athens. The presence of Laet was having a baleful influence on everyone.

'You need money to pay for the chorus and the costumes and everything. The city only gives you funds if you're the right sort of person.'

'Right sort of person?'

'Not the grandson of a slave and son of an oarsman.'

'Oh.'

They sat in silence. In the peace of the night they could hear the tide lapping around the harbour outside. Metris smiled.

Uniquely in the city, the nymph was unaffected by Laet. Her good humour had not dimmed.

'It would be so good if you could do the reading before Aristophanes' play. Maybe you could ask him again?'

Luxos shook his head. 'He'll never give me that spot. He's already offered it to Isidoros.'

'Then what about one of the other comic poets? They might let you read before their play is staged. Or maybe Eupolis needs a good lyric interlude?'

Luxos looked thoughtful. His frown eased. 'That's not a bad idea. Maybe I've been wasting my time with Aristophanes. He is a fellow Pandionis, but it's not like he's ever been that helpful. I should offer my services to Eupolis and if he says no I could try Leucon and Cratinus.'

Metris ran her fingers through his tousled blond hair.

'Why did you do that?' asked Luxos.

'I just felt like it.' Metris embraced him, and they lay down together on the small bed, an ancient item which, Luxos noticed, had never felt as comfortable as it did when he lay there with Metris in his arms.

Bremusa

Outside, it was stifling. As if Helios himself had decided to add to the city's problems, the sun blazed overhead making it far too hot for the time of year. It added to the general unhappiness. In the small shrine at the harbour, Bremusa spoke to the Goddess Athena through her altar.

'You were right, they're trying to kill Aristophanes. I can't believe there's so much fuss over a play.'

'Peace is a grave matter in Athens these days.'

'Isn't he meant to be a comedian?'

'Yes,' said the goddess. 'But nowadays Aristophanes does like to think of himself as a man with a message. Really, I preferred his earlier, funny work.'

'I can't stand him. You know I had to give him a place to sleep last night because he was too drunk to get home? It's outrageous. I'm an Amazon. It's against my sacred Amazon creed for a man to spend the night in my room.'

'It's not, actually. You just made that up.'

'Well, I still don't like it.' Bremusa ached from sleeping on the floor. It was another annoyance. Too much time in a comfortable mansion on Mount Olympus had made her soft.

'I'm afraid I'm not doing much good here, Goddess. Laet is causing chaos all over the city and I don't know how to stop her.'

'Is the nymph Metris unable to calm things down?'

Bremusa laughed bitterly. 'Metris? She spends all her time with Luxos. She claims they're in love.'

Athena was annoyed. 'I didn't send her to Athens to fall in love.'

Aristophanes

After Callias's symposium Aristophanes had his worst hangover since Alcibiades' twenty-first birthday celebration, a momentous forty-eight hours of overindulgence which had gone down in legend. He was late for rehearsal, and the people bustling around made him feel nauseous.

'Sorry I'm late, Hermogenes, I have a hangover worthy of Dionysus himself.'

He told a junior assistant to bring him a hangover cure. 'And if Luxos appears, poke him with a spear.'

'Good time at Callias's symposium?' asked Hermogenes.

'Mostly good. Didn't end so well.'

'I'm glad you've finally arrived. We're just about to rehearse the scene where the giant statue of the Peace Goddess is hauled out of the cave, flanked by the beautiful maidens, Harvest and Festival.'

Aristophanes nodded, winced, reminded himself not to nod again while he had a hangover, then followed Hermogenes over to the stage. He was eager to see what the prop-makers had come up with. For a successful comedy at the Dionysia, good props were vital. The flying beetle was an excellent start, but they needed more. The rehearsal space contained a rough replica of the stage they'd be using, with a small building in the back, and a trapdoor towards the front. Both could be used in various ways, and for this scene the trapdoor represented the mouth of an underground cavern. It was undecorated at the moment, but when the play was staged they'd put rocks and branches around it for better effect.

In *Peace*, after Trygaeus flew to heaven on the giant dung beetle, he seized the chance to rescue the Goddess of Peace from a cave, where she'd been trapped by War. All the Athenians onstage at the time, represented by the eighteen-man chorus, were to pull her out of the cave at the end of a rope. At the theatre there was a mechanism for raising objects hidden beneath the stage so they appeared through the trapdoor. It was an impressive effect, if the company got it right. When the Goddess of Peace emerged through the trapdoor, freed by honest Athenians, Aristophanes was expecting it to create quite an impression. As he arrived at the stage, the chorus had finished their dialogue and were straining mightily on the rope. At least they were meant to be. Aristophanes wasn't convinced there was a lot of straining going on.

'Put some effort into it!' he said. 'Make the audience think you're working!'

As the chorus weren't professionals, but ordinary citizens recruited for the Dionysia, it made life a little harder for Aristophanes. He couldn't yell at them in quite the way he'd have liked. They set to it well enough, however, and gave a reasonable impression of men straining to pull something heavy from the ground. The trapdoor opened. With a final, mighty effort, the chorus pulled the Goddess of Peace from the cave. Or at least they would have, if the Goddess of Peace was actually a shabby children's doll, no more than ten inches tall.

Aristophanes stared at the pathetic little artefact.

'Hermogenes, what is that?'

'Our statue.'

'But it's a child's doll.'

'I know, but it's all we've got.'

'What do you mean "it's all we've got"? You told me the statue-maker was sending over the real one today.'

Hermogenes shrugged. 'He sent a note saying he wasn't letting us have it till we paid him.'

'This is no good! I can't send my chorus onstage with a child's doll for a statue! The audience will riot.'

Aristophanes' head was pounding. 'I feel dreadful. For a rich man, I'm not certain Callias serves good quality wine. What the Hades are we going to do about this statue?'

Hermogenes looked hopeless. 'Can you pay the statue-maker?'

'No.'

'In that case, I don't know.'

'What sort of assistant are you? Find a solution!'

Hermogenes was too competent to be bullied. He stood his ground, informing Aristophanes that as writer and director, it was his responsibility to make sure the play was well enough funded by their producer. Aristophanes scowled at him. Hermogenes was right. The playwright felt like exploding in anger at everyone on stage, but realised there wasn't any point. It wouldn't help, and it would only make his hangover worse.

'Well where are the beautiful maidens that are meant to accompany the statue?' he growled.

Hermogenes pointed to two male actors, both in poor physical shape, wearing very unconvincing female costumes and masks.

Aristophanes shuddered. 'Is everything in this production designed to humiliate me?' He looked round for the junior assistant. 'Didn't I ask you to bring something for a hangover? Stop dawdling!'

He turned to Hermogenes. 'We can't put the play on like this. We'll never get out of the theatre alive. You know what a drunken rabble that audience is. By the end of the festival all standards of decency will have disappeared. Have you ever been hit by an onion thrown from the back row where the sailors' wives sit? I have. I don't intend to let it happen again.'

'Then you probably shouldn't look at the latest phalluses,' said Hermogenes. Aristophanes looked over to where two gloomy-faced actors were trying, unsuccessfully, to erect their fourteen-inch penises. There was something obscenely hopeless in the way they were working the drawstrings inside their tunics, to little effect. And not, reflected Aristophanes bitterly, obscenely hopeless in a funny way. He shuddered again. The junior assistant arrived back at a run, carrying a goblet.

'Your hangover cure.'

'Fine. Now bring me some wine, and make it quick.'

The Assembly

Hyperbolus met Euphranor before they entered the assembly. They talked quietly, standing a little aside from the mass of white-clad Athenians making their way inside. Some distance away, lines of Scythian archers were walking down the main streets carrying ropes daubed with red paint. It was a crime to miss the democratic assembly. All male citizens were obliged to attend. Anyone tardy enough to turn up with red paint on their tunic was liable to a fine.

'Something went wrong,' said Euphranor. 'Aristophanes survived.'

'Whose fault was that?'

'The assassin's, I suppose,' said the weapon-maker.

'Where did we hire him?'

'Through the priestess Kleonike.'

Hyperbolus scowled; he looked fierce, with his shaggy black hair and beard. It was an expression he often wore while speaking at the assembly. 'So we're depending on a woman now?'

Euphranor mopped his brow. The heat was overpowering. 'She's done all right for us so far. The peace conference is falling apart.'

'I suppose that's true.' Hyperbolus nodded. 'Once I've spoken in the assembly today it's going to fall apart a lot quicker. I'm going to accuse Nicias of taking bribes.'

'Has he been?'

'Who cares? Damned aristocrat, I'll see him ostracised before I'm finished with him.'

They were interrupted by two citizens, both elderly, who wanted to thank Hyperbolus for the food he'd sent them. The democratic faction had been organising the collection and distribution of supplies for impoverished citizens, and the elderly pair were grateful for the help they'd received. Hyperbolus accepted their thanks politely, and wished them well as they made their way into the assembly.

The heat was oppressive, far too hot for April. No one could remember the temperature rising so sharply before. The mood was sombre, with undertones of anger. Everyone knew that their situation was becoming desperate, and the meeting was likely to be stormy. No one expected it to end in any sort of agreement. The atmosphere in Athens had worsened quite dramatically in the past few days. Nothing was going well, and nobody could agree on anything. None of those assembled expected today's meeting to be any different to the last. Hyperbolus would hurl abuse at Nicias, accusing him of cowardice, corruption and selling out the city to the Spartans. Nicias would in turn lacerate Hyperbolus and his associates, till it seemed an absurd notion that the Athenians could ever sign a treaty with Sparta, when they themselves were so bitterly divided.

Bremusa

Bremusa had become used to the odd looks she received while walking round Athens. Although upper-class Athenian women tended to remain indoors, out of public view, there were plenty of women on the streets – vendors, tavern employees, dock workers, hetaerae, slaves and others. None looked like the Amazon. Her hair was longer, and she wore it loose and unstyled. She had dark leather armour and leggings. The leggings alone were enough to mark her out as a barbarian. No Athenian of either sex would ever wear trousers. They were the mark of the uncivilised.

After a few days, though, it did seem to Bremusa that she was receiving less attention. Perhaps people were becoming used to her. Or perhaps they had more pressing matters to worry about. The atmosphere of frustration and annoyance was tangible. It was more than just the despair caused by the never-ending war, and the failure to make progress in the negotiations. Something else was weighing Athens down. Bremusa knew that Laet's baleful influence was permeating the city.

The woman is a curse. I've never encountered anything like it. If she continues roaming around like this, something very bad is going to happen.

Bremusa looked for Metris. It took a while to locate her, but eventually she came across her at the entrance to the Long Walls that ran down to Piraeus. She was sitting with two children, amusing them by making daisies and buttercups appear beneath their feet. The children looked happy. At least someone in Athens was.

'Hello, Bremusa! I've been playing with my new friends. This is Plato, he's nine, and Xenophon, he's eight. We've been having a picnic.'

They looked like a grubby, unintelligent pair of children to Bremusa, though they did seem happier than the last time she'd encountered them, when they'd been fighting on the beach. She noticed their nanny, slumbering peacefully on a bench nearby.

'Athena wants to see you.'

From the tone of Bremusa's voice, it should have been obvious that Metris was in trouble, but the nymph was too impervious to the world around her to notice. It didn't occur to her that the goddess might be angry with her.

'All right,' she said, cheerfully. She looked down at her companions.

'I'll see you again later. We can play some more.'

Plato and Xenophon waved goodbye to their new friend. Bremusa had to admit that she'd rarely seen happier-looking children than those two at that moment. The nymph obviously did have some powers of spreading contentment. If only she could apply herself, she might be able to do something to thwart Laet, or at least ameliorate the effect of her malign influence.

When they arrived at the private shrine, the goddess herself appeared. Metris greeted her as cheerfully as a woman meeting a friend for a pleasant shopping trip.

'Thanks for sending me to Athens! I do so like it here!'

The Goddess Athena glared at her. 'What's this I hear about you and this Luxos the poet?'

'He's really nice!' enthused the nymph. 'He has lovely blond hair and he writes beautiful poems.'

The goddess was not impressed by either the lovely hair or the beautiful poems. 'Didn't I instruct you assist Bremusa?'

'I needed to comfort Luxos. He was upset after—'

'Silence! You're not there to comfort Luxos, you're there to help bring peace!'

Metris fell silent, for the first time realising that all was not well. She looked a little abashed.

'Sorry, Goddess.'

Athena leaned forward. 'Metris, listen well. You are to stay with Bremusa and assist her. You must have no more distractions. I forbid you to see Luxos again.'

Metris quailed. 'But—'

'Enough! Now do as I say! Apply yourself to the task I set you or I'll make you regret it.'

Metris was upset as they left the shrine. Bremusa was pleased. It was time someone talked some sense into the young fool.

Aristophanes

Another complete waste of time. Aristophanes rested his head on his hands as he sat in the open-air meeting place, while politicians and demagogues rose to harangue each other. He still felt queasy from his drinking exploits. He wished he were back at rehearsals. There were so many things he needed to attend to. The last rehearsal had been a shambles. It was customary for three actors to share the speaking roles in Athenian comedies, changing their masks as necessary to represent different characters. This could make it difficult for them to learn their lines but up till now that hadn't been a problem in this production. While everything else had gone wrong, Philippus and his two fellow processionals had at least managed to learn the script.

Unfortunately, they'd now forgotten it again. Aristophanes had watched, anguished, as each actor stumbled over their lines, finally grinding to a complete halt, wondering who was meant to speak next, and what they were meant to say.

'You knew these lines yesterday!' raged Aristophanes.

'Sorry.' Philippus had the good grace to look embarrassed. 'They've just completely gone out of my head. Something strange in the air in Athens these days. My art is suffering.'

'I'll make his art suffer,' muttered Aristophanes, now slumped in the baking heat. 'I'll make them all suffer. We'll have a speed run through the script at dawn tomorrow. That'll teach them to forget their lines. Great Zeus, that sun is hot. I wish I could get out of here.'

Unfortunately, the assembly lasted even longer than usual. In between all the arguing about the failing peace conference, there was a report from Delos, one of Athens' allies. They were asking for help but Athens didn't seem to be in a position to help anyone at the moment. Or if they were, no one could agree how to go about it. The failure to agree on any means to assist their ally caused more bad feeling.

There was one other item on the agenda. The ancient Altar of Pity had split in two. News of this had already spread. Though the altar was not a major place of worship in comparison to the city's great temples, it was a well-known site, and did have a place in the city's heritage. The chairman of the committee responsible for public worship reported that it had most likely just fallen apart with age, and would be repaired from public funds. He urged people not to regard it as a bad omen, but most people did exactly that. Some of the more emotional citizens declared that the city was cursed, and that neither Zeus nor Athena would ever show mercy on them again.

Aristophanes found the news about the altar more depressing than anything else. He'd secretly harboured thoughts about saying a prayer there himself, even though, strictly speaking, a failing play would not be regarded as the sort of serious problem normally taken to the Altar of Pity.

Might have been worth a shot anyway, he thought, morosely. *Nothing else is working.*

When the assembly was finally over, he tried to escape without anyone noticing him, but Nicias waylaid him outside the exit. For a man who'd just been denounced as a traitor who was taking bribes from the Spartans, Nicias seemed quite even-tempered. Aristophanes supposed he was used to it. He'd been involved in Athenian politics for a long time, and had learned how to keep an even temper. Even the malaise that had settled over the city seemed to be affecting him less than others.

'These meetings are getting worse,' sighed the politician.

'Don't give up. The population wants peace, no matter what Hyperbolus and Lamachus say.'

'Really? You'd be hard-pressed to tell that from today's assembly. It's like they've all gone insane. What happened to drive everyone mad?'

'I don't know. Perhaps the gods really do have it in for us this time.'

Nicias looked concerned. A few of his supporters tried to get his attention, but he brushed them away, maintaining his grip on Aristophanes' arm.

'There's not much time left,' he told the playwright. 'The peace conference is meant to end on the last day of the festival. We have to make this city enthusiastic about peace again. If the population don't want it, the delegates won't either. No one is going to risk his neck by signing an unpopular treaty.'

He looked Aristophanes in the eye. 'I need your play to go well.'

'I doubt my play will make any difference.'

'It advocates peace, doesn't it?'

'Yes, but ...' Aristophanes raised his hands hopelessly. 'It's not looking good.'

'Why not?'

'No money. And maybe I'm a poor writer anyway.'

Nicias was surprised. 'I counted you as one of the vainest men in Athens. Since when did you lack confidence?'

'I don't know. Nothing seems right these days.'

The politician regarded him sternly. 'Aristophanes, you can't give up as well. I need your support. Your play has to be good.'

Aristophanes departed, buying a honey cake in the agora. It was tasty as always. If the honey cakes ever declined in quality, he'd know the end was imminent. He wondered about visiting Theodota. Generally one had to make an appointment. What if she was busy, and wouldn't let him in? That was a depressing thought.

'Becoming so obsessed with the most popular hetaera in Athens probably wasn't a great idea,' Aristophanes mumbled to himself. Suddenly he felt a great desire for the comfort of another honey cake, and went back to buy more.

Luxos

Next door to Luxos's tiny shack was another home, equally humble, occupied by two elderly sisters. They lived alone, their families having been wiped out by the plague some years ago. With no means of support, they relied on charity from their tribes to see them through. Unfortunately this system was not working as well as it had done in the past. The ten tribes of Athens did their best to look after all members in need, but these days there was not enough to go round. Hyperbolus and his faction had stepped in to help, providing food for people in the poorest areas. Luxos had partaken of their charity in the past but today, feeling that the feast he'd eaten at Callias's symposium would keep him going for a while, he took the food he collected from the distribution point near the Sanctuary of Theseus to the sisters.

After dropping off the supplies, he played his lyre for them. They were grateful for the food, and they enjoyed the music.

'You've really improved with the lyre, Luxos.'

'You should sing for all the people.'

'I will one day!'

Bremusa

Bremusa was standing on the steps of the Parthenon in the company of a sullen nymph, wondering what to do next. A procession was approaching. Part of the Dionysia, she supposed, though she didn't know what part. Bremusa found the different festival activities confusing, and didn't understand what it all meant.

Metris was winding strands of her curly, dark hair round her fingers.

'Are you intending to spend all your time sulking now Athena has forbidden you to see Luxos?'

'Maybe.'

'Well, don't. We need to work.'

Metris pouted. Bremusa found that annoying. She had never pouted. Among the Amazons, it had not been encouraged.

'You dragged me to Athens on false pretences,' said the nymph.

'What are you talking about? Everything was clearly explained to you.'

'No one said I couldn't talk to poets with nice blond hair.'

'It's interfering with our mission.'

'What mission?'

Bremusa tapped her foot on the ground. The procession was coming closer. People were banging drums.

'Our mission to stop Laet.'

'Is it that important?'

'Of course it's important! It's the whole reason we're here!'

Metris was still pouting. 'I thought I was being taken to Athens to have a nice time at the festival and then I was going to live on Mount Olympus and be a goddess.'

The Amazon warrior glared at her. 'Are all nymphs as insane as you? No one is making you a goddess! That was never on the agenda.'

'Then I'm going to sulk.'

Bremusa opened her mouth, but struggled for words. She tapped her foot on the ground again, now in time with the drumming. 'And no one said anything about having a nice time either!'

'How could anyone not have a nice time at the Dionysia Festival?'

'All you've done is hang around the harbour with that stupid poet!'

'That's not true,' replied Metris. 'I've seen lots of culture with Luxos.'

'Like what?'

The young nymph started counting off things on her fingers. 'I went to the Parthenon and Luxos explained the story of the frieze to me. I saw pictures painted by Zeuxis and Parrhasius in the gallery, and then I watched a wrestling match and a running race at the stadium. Luxos took me to watch a big festival parade, and then we went to the theatre to see a tragedy by Sophocles which was really sad. Then we looked at all Phidias's most famous sculptures. We listened to Socrates talking about philosophy, and Theodorus of Cyrene lecturing about mathematics. Then Luxos took me to the docks to see how ships are made. Afterwards we met some potters and saw how they make these lovely big amphoras, and then we all went to a tavern and drank wine and sang songs. I've had a wonderful time. There's so much in Athens!'

Bremusa looked at her blankly. Metris had done all that?

'Haven't you seen any of it?' asked the nymph.

Bremusa continued to look at her blankly. She didn't know what to say. All the self-doubts she'd felt since entering Athens returned in a rush. She was an ignorant barbarian who didn't know anything about culture. She didn't even realise there was so much of it going on.

While I've been tramping the streets with a sword, Metris has apparently been studying the city's finest works of art.

The nymph was looking at her, waiting for an answer, but Bremusa was completely stuck for a reply. She didn't know what to say, and felt inadequate. She told herself not to feel inadequate. It didn't do any good. She was rescued from her humiliation by the appearance of Aristophanes, who walked morosely towards them, his head down, muttering to himself. He looked older than his years.

'I detest this city. And all the other cities. And the theatre. And people.'

'What's the matter with you?' Bremusa barked at him.

'Rehearsals are going badly. Not that it's any of your business, strange archaic woman.'

'Strange archaic woman who saved your life.'

'You did? My memory is hazy ...'

'I'm not surprised, with all that wine inside you.'

'Merely the normal imbibing of an Athenian gentleman,' said Aristophanes.

'Or a drunk. Which seems to be much the same thing. So what's wrong with rehearsals anyway?'

'No funds, terrible actors, poor chorus, talentless choreographer, incompetent musicians, useless prop-makers—'

'Maybe you have some script problems?' said Bremusa, pointedly.

'No, the writing is remarkably good. But even that can't lift this disaster of a play above the general malaise that hangs over Athens.'

Not far from them, an argument broke out in the festival procession.

'Hey, stop pushing me!'

'You trod on my foot!'

The citizens were dressed in the best clothes for the procession. It didn't stop them from shoving and jostling each other. It seemed as if blows might be landed, till a parade official managed to separate them.

'Does everyone in this city just argue all the time?' asked Bremusa.

'We do have a talent for it,' admitted Aristophanes.

The procession drew up in front of the Parthenon. A man in robes emerged to address the people. Bremusa didn't know who it was.

'That's the Archon Basileus,' said Metris. 'The chief religious official.'

'Right.' The Amazon was still smarting from the revelation that, compared to the nymph, she was an uneducated, uncultured yokel. She tried to shake the feeling off. There was important work to be done.

'Look, Aristophanes, I don't regard writing comedies as a fit occupation for a man. But somehow your play has become important to the city. So get back to your theatre and make it work.'

'No point. Without more funds, *Peace* can't go on.'

'Then get some funds.'

'Impossible. The only people with money are the weapon-makers, and they're not going to support me.'

'What about Theodota?'

Aristophanes shook his head. He was starting to go grey already. 'I can't borrow from a hetaera. That would be the most humiliating thing imaginable.'

'So? Take the humiliation. You want to win the play competition, don't you?'

'Desperately.'

'How desperately?'

'I'd sell my own grandmother.'

For the first time, Bremusa felt a slight stirring of sympathy for Aristophanes. She admired the will to win.

'Then you know what you have to do.'

For a few moments they looked into each other's eyes.

'I'll visit Theodota,' he said, then turned and walked off.

Metris giggled. 'He likes you, you know.'

'What?'

'He's attracted to you.'

'That's the most foolish thing I've ever heard, even from you.'

'I can tell,' said Metris, blithely. 'Because I'm a nymph. You should get together with him. Like a holiday romance.'

Bremusa scowled at her. 'I liked it better when you were sulking.'

Luxos

With the sun high overhead, Luxos marched through Athens, a determined expression on his face. Most of the playwrights rehearsed in the same area, and Luxos planned to visit them all if necessary. He strode up to a gate marked Private.

'I'm here to see Eupolis,' he announced to the doorman.

The guard at the entrance looked down at Luxos's long hair and shabby tunic, and his cheap sandals, which had obviously been repaired many times.

'Who are you?'

'I'm Luxos the poet.'

'Ah.' The doorman nodded. 'Then you can't come in.'

'But I want to see Eupolis.'

'Eupolis left strict instructions that no one called Luxos was ever to be allowed into his rehearsal space.'

Luxos blinked. 'Really?'

'Yes.'

'He actually named me?'

'Yes.'

'Oh.' Luxos drew himself up, which made little difference as the huge doorman still towered over him. 'Then I shall offer my services to Leucon instead. There's a poet with some taste who will appreciate my work.'

Luxos walked off. It was odd that Eupolis had actually barred him from entering.

Someone must have been spreading stories about me, he thought. *I bet it was Aristophanes.*

Luxos thought some mean thoughts about Aristophanes. It occurred to him, as he walked towards Leucon's rehearsal space, that Aristophanes' comedies were generally funnier than Leucon's. Luxos had laughed a lot last year at *The Wasps.*

But humour isn't everything, he thought. *The beauty of the poetry is important too.*

It struck him immediately that Aristophanes' poetry was better too. He used language better than Leucon.

Well I need employment somewhere, thought Luxos, *carrying on. I know these poets hire helpers to tidy up their verse, even if they don't like to admit it.*

He patted the Herm statue on the corner for luck, and approached the gate at Leucon's. There were two doormen this time, both large. As Luxos approached they became excited.

'It's him!'

'Luxos is here!'

'Eh ... hello,' said Luxos.

The doormen looked at each other.

'Leucon warned us this day would come,' said one to the other.

The doormen squared up to the small figure of Luxos. 'Begone, renegade poet. The talented and erudite Leucon does not require assistance from a skinny urchin from the slums of Piraeus!'

'But I just—'

Luxos stopped in mid-sentence, knowing it was hopeless. Apparently every established dramatic poet in Athens had been warned about him.

They all think I'm a joke.

The realisation brought with it an abrupt depression. He turned round and walked sadly away. He wished that Metris were around. He longed to see her. But apparently she was forbidden to see him now. She was off somewhere with that strange foreign woman, and wasn't allowed to visit him.

Luxos hung his head. Is it really that stupid for a poor person in Athens to try and write poetry? Hesiod wasn't rich. He was just a farmer. People gave him a chance. They let him enter competitions and he proved how good he was.

Head bowed, he tucked his lyre under his arm and trudged off home, depressed and close to defeat.

Perhaps I should just stop writing poetry. No one wants to listen. Maybe I'm no good at it anyway.

Close to home, he passed a group of young girls, playing on one of the many rough patches of vacant land around the docks. He paused to watch as five of the little girls sang a song while they danced around another girl, seated in the centre.

> *Torti-tortoise,*
> *Sitting on the ground*
> *Torti-tortoise,*
> *We're all around*
> *Weave a web of*
> *Milesian wool*
> *How did your son die?*
> *He jumped in a pool!*

As the children chanted the last line, the girl in the middle leapt up, trying to catch one of the others. There was a lot of shrieking and laughter, as whoever was caught became the new tortoise in the middle. The girls, all grubby from the rough ground, were completely involved in their play and paid no attention to Luxos.

Luxos smiled at the familiar children's game. He'd played torti-tortoise when he was an infant. He'd sung the song, too. No one knew what the words meant any more. Who had been weaving a web of Milesian wool, and whose son had jumped in a pool, was lost in history, or myth, but the rhyme could still be heard all over Athens, when children played their jumping and chasing game.

Luxos felt a little heartened. He walked home, humming 'Torti-tortoise'.

Good poetry is inspiring and it makes people happy, he thought, remembering the children's smiling faces. *I'm not giving up. Athens needs me.*

Aristophanes

Theodota's taste was widely admired. She was so wealthy that she could have built the largest house in Athens if she'd wanted. Rejecting such ostentation, she lived in the third largest. It was a notable dwelling. Her private courtyard contained a statue of Apollo that would not have looked out of place in one of the city's better temples. There were frescos on the walls painted by some of Greece's finest artists, and her collection of pottery was staggering, second only to her collection of clothes. For a twenty-four-year-old woman who was born poor, and had moved at a young age to a city that didn't grant that many rights to women, it was all quite an achievement.

'Theodota's worked for her success,' acknowledged Aristophanes, as he approached her house. 'She's used her beauty, discretion and intelligence to build up a client list of the wealthiest men in the city.'

Her clients weren't just Athenians. Theodota had received visits from famous figures from other cities too. Other countries, even.

As a hetaera, Theodota would not have been welcomed in the house of any respectable Athenian. No well-born Athenian woman would even talk to her. Her profession had put her far beyond the bounds of polite society. Aristophanes wasn't certain how she felt about that. If she took note of the poor Athenian women in the agora, working long hours for little pay, he doubted it bothered her that much.

He announced himself at the door, having sent word that he was on his way. He hoped that no one was visiting. Even when Theodota wasn't working, she did receive many callers. A surprising collection of artists, poets, philosophers, statesmen and writers could often be found there. The servant at the door welcomed him in, not that respectfully. Theodota's servants, having such a rich mistress, tended to be sniffy about her guests. Even her slaves were known to be arrogant.

'Is Theodota on her own?'

'No. The mistress is being painted by Zeuxis.'

'Oh.'

Aristophanes hadn't known that Zeuxis was painting Theodota. It wasn't really a surprise. He was one of the most famous painters in Greece. He came from the Greek colony in Heraclea, and had studied under Apollodorus.

'I'll ask her if you can observe, if you wish.'

He followed the servant through several long corridors towards one of the numerous reception rooms. Inside, Theodota was reclining naked on a couch. The afternoon light streamed in through the open window, illuminating her. Zeuxis stood at an easel, brush in hand. He was quite an unconventional character.

Mid-forties, but with longer hair than you'd expect, and a very unusual silver necklace. Artists could get away with that sort of thing, if they were famous.

Aristophanes wasn't pleased to find Socrates reclining on another couch, observing. He greeted the philosopher stiffly, Zeuxis a little less stiffly, and smiled at Theodota. Theodota smiled back at him. She wasn't at all self-conscious about being naked in company.

'Aristophanes, we were just finishing for the day.'

Zeuxis put down his brush. 'Ah, Theodota. I never thought I'd find a model beautiful enough for my painting of Helen of Troy.'

Aristophanes didn't like the way they were smiling at each other. He wondered if Zeuxis had become her lover. He felt a pang of jealousy, adding to his annoyance about Socrates being here. The man got everywhere.

Theodota motioned for a servant to bring her a robe.

'If you wait in the next room I'll join you soon,' she said.

Aristophanes waited with Socrates in another of Theodota's elegant reception rooms, of which there were many. On a shelf by the window were two vases, painted by Euphronios. In the fifty or so years since his death, Euphronios's work had become so famous in Athens that his plates, vases and amphoras were now priceless collector's items. Families who were lucky enough to own them, old Athenian families with roots deep in the past, wouldn't let them out of their sight. Even a man as rich as Callias wouldn't be able to get hold of many of them. Yet here were two of them, just sitting on a shelf in Theodota's reception rooms.

Aristophanes studied the vases for a few minutes. One depicted a courtesan, another a satyr. They were beautiful pieces of work. Euphronios deserved his reputation. Socrates was staring into space. As ever, he was dressed in the plainest homespun chiton, and a pair of leather sandals that had seen better days. Aristophanes asked him what he was doing there.

'Theodota invited me to observe the famous Zeuxis at work.'

'Oh. She never invited me. It's strange the way Theodota likes you so much. And annoying.'

'Why is it annoying?' asked Socrates.

'Because I've paid out a lot of money to her and you never pay her anything!'

'We have different expectations. I admire Theodota for her intelligence.'

'Trust you to be the only person in Athens who admires her for that.'

Socrates smiled genially. 'Zeuxis is a fine painter. I'd say his technique rivals even that of Parrhasius.'

'Parrhasius? Has he been here as well?'

Parrhasius was another very famous artist. Aristophanes knew he shouldn't have been annoyed by the way Greece's most brilliant artists flocked to Athens to paint Theodota, but he was. He suspected that his own fame as a playwright was the only reason she acknowledged him at all, and he wasn't as famous as Zeuxis or Parrhasius. He could see himself being forced out of the picture if they stayed around.

'Are they in love with her?' he asked, which was a highly inappropriate question, and one at which Socrates would have been quite entitled to laugh. He didn't.

'I couldn't say. They might be. Or they might just be here because she's one of the few people in Athens with enough money to pay their fees these days.'

A servant appeared, beckoning them through to a dining room which faced south, and was always light and airy. Theodota, now dressed, was sitting at a table laden with bowls of fruit and bread. An amphora of wine was resting on a smaller table. Aristophanes greeted her as naturally as he could, but in truth he was apprehensive. He'd come on a delicate matter, and finding Zeuxis and Socrates here had put him off his stride. At least Zeuxis seemed to have departed. He wondered if either Zeuxis or

Parrhasius had managed to catch the blue of Theodota's eyes properly. No one had eyes as blue as Theodota.

Perhaps it wasn't so bad that Socrates was here. He could be tactful, when required. If it all went humiliatingly wrong with Theodota, he'd probably manage to say something to make things less awkward. He had on one occasion rescued Aristophanes from an embarrassing moment concerning Nicias's wife, when the playwright had put his foot in it with a comment about the poor quality of the wine on offer. He hadn't known her father owned the vineyard.

'So, Aristophanes.' Theodota smiled. 'I wasn't expecting you today.'

Aristophanes wondered if either painter had managed to capture her smile. He doubted it. Theodota's smile could not be reproduced.

'Theodota, I wanted to ask you something, but ... eh ... the thing is ... hmm ... it's a little embarrassing ...'

Theodota looked amused. 'Feel free to speak your mind, Aristophanes. I started in my profession at a young age, and it would be very difficult to shock me.'

'I need to borrow a lot of money.'

Greatly shocked, Theodota had a coughing fit as some wine went down the wrong way, and she had to be assisted by her servants. There was quite a long delay while she was patted on the back and brought back to life. A young servant was sent off to fetch soothing oils.

Aristophanes shrank in his seat. *That went worse than I expected. I've almost killed her.*

Finally Theodota regained the power of speech. 'You want to borrow money? Aren't you wealthy?'

'I was, before the war. These days I'm poor like everyone else. My choregos Antimachus is starving me of funds. He doesn't like that I'm writing about peace. He doesn't want a comedy about the war ending to be successful.'

Aristophanes looked hopefully at Theodota. 'But you, as an intelligent woman, will be eager to see an end to the fighting.'

'Why? It's good for my business. When the rich men of Athens realise that they're liable to get killed any day, they tend to turn to me for comfort.'

'That may be the case. But it's not good for the people who get killed, and the people who have their farms and businesses ruined.'

'True,' said Theodota. 'But as no one permits me, or any other woman in Athens, to have a say in politics, you can't blame me for making the best of the situation.'

She mused for a moment, then turned to Socrates. 'What do you think? Would backing Aristophanes' play really help end the war?'

'It's possible,' said Socrates. 'It might influence the population. The situation is finely balanced.'

Theodota nodded. She motioned to one of her young attendants, the attractive young Mnesarete, and whispered in her ear. Mnesarete departed. Theodota sipped a little wine, rather carefully after her recent distressing experience.

'Aristophanes, you remember I told you I'd been writing in my spare time?'

Mnesarete returned. She was carrying a scroll, which she handed to Theodota.

'My first draft of a comedy,' said Theodota. 'I call it *Lysistrata*. You might like it. It's rather anti-war, just like your work. Though in my play the women of Athens have a lot more say in things.'

Aristophanes was puzzled by this development, and wary. 'I'd be ... pleased to read it some time.'

'I'd like you to put it on stage. Not right away, of course. At some future festival.'

'What? I can't do that!'

'Then I won't lend you the money.'

118

'This is outrageous. Socrates, she wants me to put on her play! Tell her it's impossible.'

Socrates sometimes wore a mocking little smile which Aristophanes found particularly annoying. He was smiling now. 'I don't know that we could say it's impossible, Aristophanes. There's no logical reason why it couldn't be done.'

'There are plenty of reasons.'

'None of them insurmountable. It would have to be produced under your name, of course, but it could be done.'

'Stop supporting her!'

'It's only a first draft,' said Theodota. 'We could rewrite it together. I'd need final say, of course. And the heavy end of the box office.'

Bremusa

With Athens becoming more factious by the hour, and the signing of a peace treaty less likely every moment, Bremusa wondered if it was worth using Metris's cheerful aura to try and counteract Laet. While the nymph didn't have her mother's powers of dispelling all negative energies, it did seem to Bremusa that she had a way of improving people's moods. Not Bremusa's mood – she still found her infuriating – but other people seemed to like her. When she was happy, the nymph exuded warmth. She'd certainly cheered up the children she'd met, and other people seemed happier when she was around.

'Let's just walk through the agora and see if you can lighten the mood.'

Metris was doubtful. 'I can't counteract Laet. She's too powerful.'

'I know. But children like you. Maybe you can cheer up the market workers and make them all stop arguing. We have to do something. The goddess told me to use my initiative and I can't think of anything else.'

Metris was willing to try, but she was distracted. Bremusa knew why.

'The goddess didn't send you here to waste your time on poets of dubious talent.'

'Luxos has plenty of talent!' cried Metris.

'Talent? Ha.' Bremusa quickly changed the subject, worried that Metris might be as knowledgeable about poetry as she'd turned out to be about other Athenian arts. If the nymph started lecturing her on Homer she'd have to kill her. 'If we pay attention, we might be able to find out where Laet has been, and try improving things there.'

'I think she's been over there,' said Metris.

'Why?'

'Because that house is on fire.'

Suddenly there were Athenian citizens everywhere, rushing around with buckets, jars, amphoras, anything that would carry water.

'I told Polykarpos not to roast a whole sheep in his bedroom!' cried an elderly man. 'It was bound to go wrong.'

'We need more water!'

The amount of water the Athenians were able to produce seemed hopelessly insufficient. The flames took hold. Bremusa turned to Metris, only to find that she was no longer at her side. She'd walked over towards the firefighters. As the Amazon watched, the nymph discreetly pointed a finger. Their buckets and amphoras instantly began to fill up with water. Bremusa pursed her lips.

I suppose having a river goddess as your mother does have its advantages.

'Where did all this water come from?' cried one of the firefighters.

'Never mind, put the fire out!'

Metris rejoined Bremusa and they watched as the Athenians quickly damped down the flames, assisted by the endless supply of water that seemed to have appeared from nowhere. Metris looked smug.

'All right,' said Bremusa. 'I admit you're not so useless. Producing all that water was very effective.'

She noticed that the area around the dampened house was now blanketed with a great field of buttercups and daisies.

'They could probably have managed without all the flowers.'

'I thought it was a nice touch.'

Metris suddenly shivered. She turned towards the edge of the agora. 'But that doesn't feel very nice.'

'What?' said Bremusa. Metris was already walking towards a small altar, an ancient, almost featureless stone pillar. She came to a halt, examining it. The Altar of Pity had been repaired by the city's workmen. There were no finer stonemasons than those in Athens, and they'd done an excellent job of repairing it.

'But it's no good,' said Metris.

'What are you talking about?'

'This lovely old altar. They've repaired it but it hasn't made it right. The altar doesn't work any more. It's been spoiled.'

'How?'

'By Laet, I suppose.' Metris appeared distressed. 'It was such a beautiful old altar. Laet's ruined it.'

'Can you fix it?'

Metris shook her head. 'She's too powerful for me. I can't do anything.'

Aristophanes

Walking down the street with Socrates, Aristophanes was disconsolate.

'I'm disconsolate,' he said.

'You look disconsolate.'

'Why wouldn't I be? I don't want to put on Theodota's play.'

'You haven't read it yet. It might be good.'

'I doubt it. What sort of title is *Lysistrata*? And even if it is good, how could I use her script? The festival authorities aren't going to accept a play written by a woman. It would be a scandal.'

'Theodota knows that,' said Socrates. 'She offered to rewrite it, with you. Aren't your plays sometimes put on under your producer's name anyway?'

'Sometimes. But the whole thing is demeaning. Who's the comic genius here, me or Theodota?'

Socrates halted and looked at him. 'I don't know about comic genius but if you want to be a romantic genius, I'd be a little more enthusiastic about Theodota's talents. If you just dismiss them she'll be angry.'

'Will she?'

'Yes.'

Aristophanes sighed. 'I suppose you're right. Do you think she's been plotting this all along? Perhaps she only ever agreed to see me so that one day she could trick me into producing her play.'

Socrates laughed. 'Who knows? I told you she was intelligent. Look on the bright side. At least you've got the money you need.'

With that, Socrates departed, off to his daily practice of talking about philosophy with whoever would listen. Aristophanes headed towards his rehearsal, feeling dissatisfied about various things but relieved that at last his production had money. Theodota had provided him with all the funds he required.

'I'll show these Athenians what a comedy is meant to be. And I'll show up these warmongers in the assembly for the fools they are while I'm at it.'

Luxos

The sun blazed down. The city sweltered, and tempers rose. Athenian priests checked their records to see if it had ever been so hot during the Dionysia before, and wondered if it was another portent of misfortune.

Luxos stopped to look at some street performers in the shade of the Temple of Eukleia. Despite the heat, they were juggling, tumbling, throwing and catching hoops. He knew them slightly, and waved. They depended on whatever money they could pick up from passers-by, so he felt a sense of fellowship. Luxos was not athletic, but he did sympathise with fellow struggling artists. There was an uncomfortable gnawing in his stomach. It might have been hunger, or it might have been the realisation that he had no money and no prospects. He stood in the same spot for a long time, wishing that the street performers might divert his attention away from his sadness over Metris.

He rested against the wall of the temple. Eukleia – the spirit of glory, and good repute. 'A spirit that obviously dislikes me,' he muttered, considering the state of his own reputation.

'You look sad, Luxos.'

It was Socrates.

'My heart is broken,' announced Luxos. 'Metris isn't allowed to talk to me any more.'

'Who isn't allowing her?'

'The Goddess Athena.' Luxos looked defiantly at the philosopher. 'I expect you think I'm crazy for saying that.'

'No, I believe you.'

'You do? Oh.' Luxos was pleased, but then his face fell. 'Athena says Metris has to help with important work. She can't see me any more.'

The young poet's brow furrowed, and he began to look angry. 'It's outrageous. After all the prayers I've offered up to the goddess. And all the daisies I've left at her altar!'

A beautiful dark-haired woman appeared behind the street performers. Laet gazed at Luxos.

'I'm going to have revenge,' said Luxos to Socrates. 'I'll make Goddess Athena regret ruining my romance. I'm going to write a really mean poem about her.'

'That's your plan?'

'Yes.'

Socrates looked at Luxos, slightly raising one eyebrow.

'Why are you looking at me like that? Athena deserves to have a nasty poem written about her.'

Socrates continued to look at Luxos. Luxos stared down at his feet. He shifted uncomfortably under Socrates' gaze.

'Maybe it's not such a great idea. I'll probably just get cursed or something. And then I'll never see Metris again. But what else can I do? I can't do anything except write poetry.'

In the background, Laet had worn a faint smile, but it was fading as Luxos stood in deep thought.

'Do you think maybe it would be a good idea to write something nice about Goddess Athena?' he asked Socrates.

Socrates smiled.

'Of course,' said Luxos. 'You're right. I'm going to write a really great poem about Athena! Then she'll let me see Metris again!'

Luxos hurried off enthusiastically, turning to call back to Socrates. 'Thanks, Socrates. You're a really wise man!'

The street performers were making a human pyramid, juggling hoops as they climbed on top of each other. Idomeneus joined Laet. He gazed at the departing Luxos.

'That didn't go quite as expected,' he said.

Laet narrowed her eyes, displeased.

'Socrates' rationality triumphs over your baleful influence,' said Idomeneus.

Laet smiled, quite cruelly. 'Let Socrates have a few small triumphs. Athens will do for him in the end.'

They walked off. As they passed by the street performers Laet directed a fierce scowl in their direction. Immediately their performance went disastrously wrong and they crashed in a painful heap on the ground.

Luxos ran all the way home. He grabbed his lyre, a quill and his very last sheet of parchment. 'I'm going to write a really great poem about the Goddess Athena,' he muttered, and got to work.

Aristophanes

Aristophanes was in his element. There was nothing like the bustle of a rehearsal space when things were going well. He felt that the Goddess Athena herself might have been smiling on them as they went to work that day. Now that they had the money they needed, everything was starting to go well.

'Get that dung beetle flying up there! I want to see it swooping over the audience. That's much better! Hermogenes, have the chorus go through the last number again, I want some rhythm! Where are my new phalluses?'

'Just arrived. They're huge!'

'Do they rise properly?'

'Like mighty oak trees!'

'Excellent! This is more like it. I'll show Eupolis and Leucon how to put on a comedy. Chorus, get these phalluses strapped on and wave them like you mean it!'

A second young assistant arrived in a rush. 'We've just received a message from Isidoros. He got your payment and he's prepared to take the introductory spot.'

Aristophanes nodded approval. 'Good news. Isidoros's poetry recital will warm up the crowd. Have you heard him recently? Sensational lyre playing. And not a bad rhymer, when he's sober. Was he sober?'

'His secretary assured me he was.'

'Then let's hope for the best.'

A third second assistant hurried over. 'The new statues are here!'

A team of stagehands carried the new statue of peace onto the stage. It was a lightweight construction, made of wood, for theatrical use only, but it was beautifully carved and painted. The Goddess of Peace herself would have been delighted with it. If there were a Goddess of Peace, that was. Strictly speaking, there wasn't. But there were so many divine figures in the Athenian pantheon that creating a new one for the purposes of the play wouldn't offend anyone. As Aristophanes said, who could object to a Goddess of Peace?

'Great statue!' he enthused. 'When that pops up out of the cavern the audience can't fail to be impressed. And we'll impress them even more when young Mnesarete makes her appearance.'

Mnesarete, Theodota's servant, was currently wandering around the stage, semi-clad, rehearsing for her appearance at the end of the play. She was a beautiful young woman. The stagehands had expressed their complete approval.

Hermogenes frowned. 'Is it really necessary to send on a naked young woman?'

'Yes.'

'It still seems cheap.'

'Cheap? Who cares if it's cheap? You think these idiots on the judging panel care about art?'

Annoyingly for Aristophanes, Hermogenes wouldn't drop the subject. 'I care,' he said. 'And you used to as well. I remember when you first appeared in the theatre. All you could talk about was the quality of your poetry. You used to despise stage effects. Said they were taking away from the purity of the drama.'

'That's when I was young and stupid. You know as well as I do that the audience is never going to be satisfied with a comedy just because it has the best poetry.'

'I don't know that at all. They might be. And even if they're not, isn't that what matters to you most? It used to be.'

Aristophanes could feel a slight throbbing in his head. The heat in the open-air rehearsal space was oppressive. 'What matters to me most is winning the competition. I was swindled out of first prize last year and that's not going to happen again. Now stop sounding like Socrates and help me unload these new costumes.'

They pitched in to help the stagehands who were carrying a great mass of props and costumes into the theatre. Time was now very short, and everyone was working furiously. The actors had completed their speed run that morning, racing through their lines at a furious pace in an effort to memorise them fully, and it seemed to have worked. Philippus could now deliver his opening speech quite beautifully, and he'd even stopped complaining about the giant beetle.

'How did you pay for all this?' asked Hermogenes.

'Oh, I just called in a few favours.' Aristophanes looked thoughtful. 'Hermogenes, do you think a comedy about women ruling the city would be such a bad idea?'

Bremusa

Bremusa went to the private shrine to commune with the goddess. Once again, Athena made herself visible. She wasn't in her mansion but on the slopes of Mount Olympus, in front of a small rural altar, not much more than an ancient pile of stones.

'I've failed, Goddess. Laet is causing chaos. Everyone is making bad decisions. We'll be lucky if the whole city doesn't burn to the ground.'

'Please don't let that happen. When the Persians set fire to my temples it reduced me to tears.'

'I remember. But I don't know what to do to make things better.'

'You have to keep trying. If they manage to hold the last session of the peace conference, who knows what might happen?'

'I know what will happen. Laet will turn up and everyone will be at each other's throats.'

The goddess smiled. 'We have to hope for the best. You haven't done badly so far.'

'Goddess, could I really not just chop Laet's head off? It would make everything much easier.'

'No! I don't think she would die from your blade, Bremusa. Even if she did, Athens would be cursed. With her spirit haunting the acropolis, the city would be doomed.'

'Can I kill Idomeneus?'

'I'd rather you didn't.'

'He deserves it.'

'Why?'

'Because . . .' Bremusa paused. She couldn't really say why he deserved to die, though she wanted to kill him. He'd defeated her on the battlefield at Troy. It was an affront to her honour. She didn't want to admit that to the goddess. She shouldn't be thinking of her own desires.

'He's a bad person,' she said, limply. 'And he's protecting Laet.'

'You're there to assist the Athenians make peace, Bremusa. You should avoid violence if at all possible.'

'Would that include slapping Luxos and Metris round the head?'

The goddess laughed. 'You always pretend you're no good for anything but fighting, Bremusa. But that's not true. I know you can do more.'

'I'm an Amazon. If I don't get to fight I get twitchy.'

'If you need some activity, try sampling Athenian culture.'

Bremusa scowled. 'I don't understand culture. Even that

foolish nymph knows more than me. Metris has been looking at art behind my back. She's seen statues and paintings and processions and all sorts of things. Now I'm feeling ignorant. I'm obviously too stupid to understand culture.'

'Perhaps Aristophanes' comedy might serve as a gentle introduction?'

'I have a very poor sense of humour.'

The goddess smiled. 'Now's your chance to develop it. If Aristophanes can make the city laugh, it might go a long way to combating Laet. So take care of him.'

Bremusa sighed. 'I'll try my best.'

Luxos recites

Luxos stood alone on the beach, a solitary figure far from the city walls, declaiming to the waves. He often came here to practice. Words written down were one thing, but recitation was another. Poetry had to sound right. Here, with his lyre, facing the Mediterranean, competing with the sound of the tides and the seabirds overhead, Luxos would refine his technique, strengthening his voice, perfecting his emphasis so that the poetry flowed powerfully and gracefully. With no one to distract him, Luxos would recite for hours.

He was trying out some lines of his new poem about the Goddess Athena when he heard someone call his name. Metris was scrambling over the rocky shore towards him.

'Luxos, I'm so glad you're safe!'

'Thanks, but—'

'I had a terrible dream! I saw you dying!'

Luxos frowned. It wasn't the best thing to hear, particularly from a nymph who might well have powers of seeing things that others couldn't.

'What happened?'

'I saw you lying under a great burnt-out chariot! At least I think it was a chariot. Something with wheels, anyway. I think it might have been the future.'

'Well, I'm safe for a while then,' said Luxos. 'There aren't many chariots around here.'

'But what if you go to war? The enemy might have chariots.'

'The Spartans wouldn't. I suppose the Persians might. Were there Persians in your dream?'

Metris shook her head. 'No.' She frowned, as if trying to piece her memories of the dream together. 'I got the impression you were a long way away. Like thousands of miles. And maybe hundreds of years in the future. Someone said you had died.'

Luxos's alarm ebbed away. 'At least I'm safe for the moment.'

They sat down together. Metris carried a small canvas bag. She brought out a loaf of bread and some goat's cheese. They shared the food on the beach, sitting close so their bodies touched.

'Why would I be alive, hundreds of years in the future?'

'Who knows? Bremusa and Idomeneus have managed it. Funny things happen when you meet anyone from Mount Olympus.'

The heat was still oppressive but not quite as bad on the beach, with a breeze coming in from the sea. Despite Metris's odd premonition, Luxos's spirits had soared when she appeared.

'It's so good to see you. Will this get you into trouble with Bremusa?'

'She likes me better since I put some fires out. She gave me some time off.' Metris delicately arranged their cheese on two slices of bread. 'Listen, I had an idea. You told me Isidoros was reciting his poetry before Aristophanes' play. You said he drinks a lot?'

'He's notorious for it.'

'How about getting him drunk before he starts? If he was too

130

drunk to recite, maybe there'd be no time for Aristophanes to find anyone else? Then he'd let you go on instead.'

Luxos considered the nymph's suggestion. It wasn't a bad plan. Isidoros was famously fond of wine. He had been known to miss performances because of it. Getting him drunk on purpose was a credible idea. It might be done. And after that, who knew? Luxos might find himself the only person capable of taking his place at short notice.

He shook his head. 'I don't think I can do that.'

'Why not?'

'It wouldn't be honourable. I can't harm a fellow poet.'

'Even one you don't like?'

'I'm afraid not.'

Metris was temporarily disappointed but soon smiled again. She liked that Luxos was honourable. She put her arm round him.

'If you ever find yourself dying under a huge burnt-out chariot, hundreds of years in the future, I'll rescue you at the last moment. Anyone who says you died will be wrong. Even if people think you're dead, I'll still save you.'

'Can you do that?'

'Of course. I'm a nymph. And I'm getting really close to Athena these days. She'll probably grant me lots of new powers when she invites me to live on Mount Olympus.'

Rehearsal

It was the eve of the final day of the Dionysia. Tomorrow, the comedies would be performed and judged. Aristophanes knew his play wasn't perfect but, for the first time, he was cautiously optimistic. The whole production had been given a boost by Theodota's money. Everyone was pleased with their new props and costumes, and showed a willingness to work. Even the technical rehearsal, often a tedious process, went fairly well. Every prop was carefully tested, scenes were gone over again and again until everything ran smoothly, with all the actors and chorus doing their best to make the comedy work.

'We've done all we can,' said Aristophanes to Hermogenes. 'We might get away with it.'

Hermogenes nodded. He'd been pleased with the rehearsals, though he still worried about some technical aspects of the play. With the many tragedies and comedies all being performed at the same location during the Dionysia, the various acting companies could not rehearse at the theatre itself. At their own rehearsal space they had a replica of the stage, but that wasn't quite the same. There was always the fear that something might go wrong when they performed in the great theatre of Dionysus.

The actors, chorus, stagehands and everyone else associated with the production were warned by Aristophanes to make sure they got a good night's sleep. All of them ignored his warning, and spent the night celebrating instead, turning up at the theatre the next morning in a fragile state, but still ready to work hard.

The Final Day of the Dionysia

The delegations from Athens and Sparta were due to meet for the last time. The meeting would begin as soon as the plays were finished. If no agreement could be reached the war would continue.

Earlier in the day, Hyperbolus, Kleonike, Lamachus and Antimachus met in Euphranor's house, discreetly entering his villa via the alleyway at the back, cloaked, their faces hidden. Their meeting was tense. Euphranor addressed them with the air of a very wealthy man who was unused to his wishes being thwarted.

'When I put my money into this enterprise I was assured of success. But the peace conference is still going ahead, and so is Aristophanes' play.'

'Don't worry, Euphranor, everything's still on course,' said Hyperbolus.

The priestess Kleonike gazed out from beneath her grey, hooded cloak and spoke quite mockingly. 'It doesn't sound like everything is still on course.'

'Well maybe that creature you summoned to Athens isn't as good as you said she was! Though she cost enough.'

'Most of which I paid,' said Euphranor.

'Don't blame me,' said the priestess. 'Laet has been highly effective. All you had to do was finish things off.'

General Lamachus frowned. He'd never liked the idea of involving a priestess. 'We should never have gone down that route. Warriors trust their own strength.'

Kleonike laughed, infuriating the general.

'Enough arguing!' said Antimachus, Aristophanes' producer. 'We don't have time for it.'

'Don't you start, Antimachus, said Euphranor. 'You've failed worse than anyone. You were meant to sabotage Aristophanes and now I hear he's got everything he needs.'

'I kept my part of the bargain! I starved him of funds!'

'Then where did he get the money?'

'I don't know.'

'Well he got money from somewhere.' Hyperbolus scowled at everyone in the room. He wore his best chiton. It was a respectable garment but it didn't make him look any less intimidating. 'We've got four hours before the play begins. We have to either delay it or sabotage it. It must not go well. If the audience all start cheering for peace, it might affect the delegates.'

'How are we meant to sabotage it?' asked General Lamachus.

'Any way we can. Bribe the actors. Steal their props. Kleonike, can you send Laet down to the theatre?'

'She's already on her way.'

'Good. The play must not go on.'

Citizens Arrive at the Theatre

The Theatre of Dionysus Eleuthereus lay under the shadow of the acropolis, in the south of the city, close to a smaller theatre, the Odeon, built by Pericles, used for music and singing. It was in this smaller theatre that the proagon had been held, when the titles of the upcoming plays were announced and the judges were selected. The Theatre of Dionysus was a good deal larger, a circular, open-air space holding twelve thousand people. The acoustics were excellent, though the wooden benches were not especially comfortable, particularly for an audience who might spend the whole day there. People laid their cloaks on the benches to make it easier; wealthier citizens brought their own cushions, or hired them. Some days the theatre could be a scene of extreme emotion, as the plays of Athens' famous tragedians were performed in an atmosphere of religious reverence. On the last day of the Dionysia, the atmosphere changed to one of raucous amusement, as the comedies were staged, comedies which were famous all over Greece for their wit, obscenity and irreverence. The adult population of Athens crammed into the theatre. There were guests too, visitors to the city, and ambassadors from foreign states. Notably, there were representatives from the other Greek states which paid Athens tribute in exchange for protection.

As Nicias made his way to the theatre, he noticed the atmosphere was more subdued than at previous festivals. Perhaps that was to be expected, given the difficult times Athens had been going through recently. The unseasonal heat had not dissipated, and people were feeling it. There was anxiety too. Everyone seemed to know someone who'd been involved in recent misfortune, from merchants who'd lost money on deals, to women who'd lost their lives in childbirth. It had been the unluckiest month anyone could remember, and no matter what a citizen did to make things better, it always went wrong. It was as if the city had collectively lost its ability to make the right choice in anything. It didn't bode well for the peace conference.

If the mood was less festive than usual, it was not entirely sombre. People were glad of a few days' break from worrying about the war, and listening to politicians screaming insults at each other in the assembly. Whatever might happen in the coming weeks, they were at least sure to laugh at the plays of Aristophanes, Eupolis and Leucon. People looked forward to seeing three comedies, one after another, although even that number carried a reminder of their troubles. At one time there had been five comedies, but the number had been reduced, because of the war.

Luxos

Luxos made his way to the theatre on his own. Metris had returned to her duties with Bremusa. Luxos missed her, though his spirits had been bolstered by the picnic they'd shared on the beach. He had already written twenty-eight lines about sharing their bread and cheese, and there was a lot more to come.

He'd considered boycotting the last day of the festival in protest at it not involving him in any way, but no Athenian could be truly comfortable missing out on such a huge communal event.

I'll just have to sit through that hack Isidoros reciting his useless poetry. I will watch with dignity. Maybe mutter a little abuse. Nothing extravagant.

135

He wondered how Aristophanes' play would be received. Luxos had seen a lot of it in rehearsal. None of it seemed to be working that well, though he could see its potential if it all came together. Recent events had not endeared Aristophanes to Luxos. Nonetheless, the young poet wanted the war to end. If Aristophanes' play could help, then he probably should support it.

Luxos was swept up in the great mass of citizens approaching the theatre. For a short time he experienced the feeling of unity, of commune, of being part of a great body of people all striving for the same thing: the Athenians, proud of their city, and their democracy, and their arts. It was spoiled when three youths, part of a wealthy family, flanked by servants, poked fun at him.

'What's that? Is that meant to be a lyre?'

'Looks like something washed up on the beach.'

'So does he.'

'Get a haircut, you look like a barbarian.'

Luxos sighed. He was used to criticism, both personal and artistic, but he wasn't immune to it. As the theatre came into view, his spirits fell further. Here he was, in the very heart of Greek culture, and he couldn't make any impression. He wished that it wasn't so hot. He wished Metris was there. He wished someone would listen to his poetry.

Aristophanes

Leucon's comedy was nearing its conclusion. It had gone well with the audience but Aristophanes wasn't paying attention. He had no regard for Leucon, and was too busy double-checking that everything was ready for his own company's performance. After their final rehearsals, Aristophanes was feeling optimistic. There would be no repeat of last year, when the panel of five judges had denied him first prize.

One of the most scandalously corrupt decisions ever seen in the Athenian theatre!

He entered the backstage area to make a final check. Hermogenes ran towards him, a look of alarm on his face.

'What's the matter?'

'Our penises have gone missing.'

Aristophanes stared at him blankly. His assistant seemed to be talking gibberish. 'What do you mean "Our penises have gone missing?"'

'I mean they've disappeared!'

'I don't understand.'

'How much clearer can I be? Our giant funny phalluses are no longer on the premises!'

'But how?'

'Someone's stolen them!'

Aristophanes looked at him, aghast. 'Not the new, big ones? Not all of them?'

'Yes!'

Aristophanes sagged. Never before in the theatre had he received such a body-blow.

'It's the end,' he muttered. Tears welled up in his eyes. He looked up to heaven. 'Why? Why do the gods curse me? Am I really such a bad person?'

He slumped into a chair. 'Cancel the play. We can't go on.'

'We can't cancel the play,' said Hermogenes. 'The play must go on. Everyone knows that. The crowd would riot.'

'But what can we do? We can't send the actors on without huge dangly penises. It's unheard of. It's probably against festival rules.'

Hermogenes shrugged 'We'll just have to use the old, small, unsatisfactory penises.'

'But they're back at the rehearsal space!'

'I'll send people to fetch them,' said Hermogenes.

'Do we have time?'

'We could ask Isidoros to recite for a little longer. He's due to go on any moment now.'

Bremusa

It was a long time since Bremusa had actually seen anyone skipping gaily along the street. It tended not to happen on Mount Olympus, and it was never done among the Amazons. Metris was, however, skipping along at that moment, bubbling over with enthusiasm.

'What are you so happy about?'

'I'm so looking forward to the comedy! It will be lovely to be in the theatre!'

'I think you're happy because you sneaked off to see Luxos.'

'No, I didn't!' Metris smiled. As a nymph, she never felt that much obligation to tell the truth, if the truth happened to be awkward.

Bremusa was trying to think of something withering to say, because the skipping was annoying her, when she practically bumped into Idomeneus of Crete. He stood, tall and rock-like in front of her, looking down on her with contempt. Behind him were two men, pulling a cart.

'Bremusa the Amazon.'

'Idomeneus of Crete.'

'I'd kill you but I'm busy at the moment.'

'I'd kill you but I'm busy too.'

The cart was covered by a tarpaulin. Metris, for no particular reason, peered under it.

'Look! It's full of big penises.'

'I told you, the city is obsessed with them,' said Bremusa. 'Let's go.'

'But they must have stolen them from Aristophanes!' cried

Metris, an astute observation that had not occurred to the Amazon. She stared at Idomeneus.

'Is that true?'

'What if it is?'

Bremusa laid her hand on the pommel of her sword. 'Hand them over.'

'No,' said Idomeneus.

'I'm not letting you ruin Aristophanes' play.'

'What do you care about the theatre?'

'I'm a huge enthusiast.' Bremusa drew her sword. 'You've lived too long, Idomeneus.'

Idomeneus drew his sword. 'Prepare to die, Amazon.'

Abruptly, shockingly, and rather absurdly, a huge wall of flowers suddenly erupted between the Amazon and the Cretan warrior. Metris had caused a giant mass of buttercups and daisies to separate them, doing it in such a way that Idomeneus and his men were on one side, while she, Metris and the cart were on the other.

'Metris, what are you doing?'

'I'm fed up with all this silly fighting. You really ought to try resolving your problems some other way. Come on, let's take these back to the theatre.'

Bremusa and Metris hurried off, pulling the cart behind them, leaving Idomeneus and his hirelings still trying to fight their way through a wall of flowers.

Aristophanes

Aristophanes mopped perspiration off his brow. The heat was oppressive in the covered backstage area.

What's keeping Hermogenes? Where's Isidoros? He should be reciting by now.

Outside in the theatre, there were murmurings. The audience were becoming restive. They didn't like to be kept waiting, not when the temperature was so high. A lot of festival wine had already been consumed. That could make an audience receptive. It could also make them hostile.

Hermogenes burst into the room. 'Isidoros can't go on.'

'What? Why not?'

'You'd better see for yourself.'

Aristophanes followed his assistant into the next room, up a flight of stairs, and along a corridor. There, in one of the dressing rooms, he was not that surprised – having already worked out that this was the most likely cause of the problem – to find Isidoros lying on a couch in a drunken stupor. The playwright looked at his prone figure with disgust.

'Didn't he promise he wasn't going to do this?' Aristophanes rounded on Hermogenes. 'You were meant to keep him sober!'

'I can't do everything! He was fine when I last saw him.'

The famous lyric poet opened his eyes and raised a limp hand in greeting to the playwright. 'Aristophanes. You're always criticising Hyperbolus. But he's a fine man. Very liberal with the wine. Always ready to give a man an amphora or two.'

With that, Isidoros closed his eyes and began to snore.

'Now what do we do?' cried Aristophanes. 'We can't start the play without our penises and we don't have Isidoros to entertain the crowd while they're waiting.'

'You'll have to stall,' said Hermogenes. 'Get out there and make excuses to the audience.'

'What sort of excuses?'

'You're the creative genius,' said Hermogenes. 'I'll see if there's any sign of the old phalluses arriving.'

Hermogenes hurried off. Aristophanes made his way pensively back along the corridor and down the stairs to the side of the stage. He felt his spirit wilting. It was all very well for Hermogenes to talk about stalling. An Athenian audience was not that easy to stall. Particularly at the end of the day, when they'd already worked themselves up by watching two comedies and drinking heavily. Anyone walking out on stage with bad news was liable to get hit by a well-aimed onion. The Athenian audience could turn nasty very quickly.

Some of these people will have drunk enough wine to sink a trireme by now, he thought. *Wine is a curse. It should be outlawed.*

He took a deep breath and walked out on stage. Already the murmurings of discontent were growing as the audience realised the play wasn't going to start on time. Aristophanes emerged through the skene, the small wooden building at the back of the stage, and made his way forward. The noise coming from the crowd was growing. The theatre was built to seat twelve thousand people, and there were more than that crammed in today, with some sitting in the aisles, and others standing at the back.

Aristophanes gazed out at the vast crowd, hoping to see a few friendly faces. Unfortunately, the only faces he could see were those of Hyperbolus, Euphranor and their friends, gathered near the front of the auditorium, no doubt for the purpose of heckling the production. He walked to the front of the stage. The heat was still intense.

'Citizens of Athens! There has been an unfortunate delay—'

That was as far as he got before the first jeers started. It struck Aristophanes that after all he'd done for the city, they might have been a little more tolerant, but apparently not. He could feel sweat trickling uncomfortably down his neck.

'We're not quite ready to begin, and our esteemed poet, Isidoros, is currently indisposed—'

This produced a great deal of mocking laughter. Isidoros's reputation was well known.

'—but we'll be starting soon. Quite soon. It's hard to say when exactly, but not too long, I would say. Almost certainly it will be not long from now . . . '

Aristophanes knew he was babbling. Hyperbolus and his claque started booing, which put him off further. A few pieces of fruit began to land on the stage.

'Aristophanes is making fools of us!' cried someone. One of Euphranor's many paid flunkies, most probably.

'Booooo!'

The barrage of fruit began to intensify. The combination of the heat, the tense atmosphere in the city, and the efforts of Hyperbolus and Euphranor to ridicule Aristophanes threatened to make events spiral out of control in record time. Aristophanes wouldn't be the first dramatist to be chased out of the Theatre of Dionysus Eleuthereus. He looked round desperately for assistance, hoping that Hermogenes might appear with news of their reserve phalluses. There was no sign of him. More vegetables began to appear onstage, including a cabbage, which could be a lethal weapon if thrown by an Athenian who'd been hardened on the battlefield.

Aristophanes tried to stall for time. 'Meanwhile, we'll be entertaining you with ... eh ... eh ... ' Unfortunately, he didn't know what they'd be entertaining them with.

'Booooo! Booooo!'

The crowd started a slow handclap. While their emotions were unusually intense, they did have cause for complaint. The city granted certain playwrights the honour of showing their work at the festival, and they had months to prepare their plays. The least the city might expect in return was that the playwrights should be ready on time. It was highly unusual for there to be such a long delay, and the audience didn't like it at all.

The slow handclap was one of the most humiliating moments of Aristophanes' life. He was on the verge of fleeing the stage. Fleeing the city, perhaps. An onion caught him in the ribs, making him wince. Hyperbolus and the agents he'd distributed around the audience were now roaring at the top of their voices, mocking Aristophanes and calling for him to be expelled from the competition. He looked round desperately for inspiration, and found none.

'We'll be ... we'll be ...'

'We'll be entertaining you with a performance from one of our most promising young lyric poets – Luxos of Piraeus!' cried Luxos, rushing on to the stage, his lyre in his hand.

Aristophanes looked at Luxos wildly. Fruit and vegetables continued to rain down. He turned to the crowd. 'Indeed! A performance from one of our most promising young poets. Please welcome Luxos!'

With that, Aristophanes fled the stage. In the wings he crashed right into Hermogenes. Hermogenes raised his eyebrows.

'Luxos? You're going to let him go through with it?'

'What else could I do?'

'They'll kill him.'

'Rather him than me.' Aristophanes shuddered.

They turned to peer out from the wings, carefully keeping themselves hidden while Luxos faced the hostile crowd.

'I really don't think this is a good idea,' said Hermogenes.

'I didn't make him invade the stage. Anyway, he wanted a chance to perform to an audience, didn't he? Now he's got one.'

The audience were now even more hostile. A performance from an unknown young poet was not what they'd come here for. Standing in front of the huge crowd in the amphitheatre, stretched out in a great semicircle all around him, Luxos looked tiny. And very shabby, Aristophanes suddenly noticed, with a pang of sympathy.

'Isn't that Luxos the oarsman's son?' shouted someone in the audience.

'What does he know about poetry?'

'Booooo! Booooo!'

An onion flew over Luxos's head, missing him by inches. Aristophanes was expecting him to flee, and wouldn't have blamed him. The young poet held his ground, even striding forward to the front of the stage. He raised his lyre, took a deep breath, and addressed the audience in a surprisingly strong, clear voice.

'Fellow Citizens of Athens – this is a poem I wrote about the Goddess Athena.'

Pallas Athena, glorious child of almighty Zeus
Righteous, blissful and blessèd goddess
Striding over mountains,
through groves and caverns
Rejoicing in mastery of sword and spear
Fierce in battle,
Strengthening weak mortal souls
With the terrible spirit of the Furies

Athletic maiden
Free from marriage
You wrath descends on the wicked
And your wisdom on the good
Raging destroyer of Gorgons and joyful Mother of the Arts

Mistress of wisdom
Master of strategy
Male, female, natures combined
Shapeshifter
Form-changer
Great-spirited dragon of war
Slayer of giants
Thundering tamer of stallions,
Destroy every evil
And bring us victory!

Goddess, Warrior, Artist,
Grey-eyed Athena
Hear our prayers, night and day,

Grant us peace, health,
Victory and wealth,
We praise you, and ask
That our lives may be ever joyful under your protection.
I dedicate this hymn to you,
Great Goddess Athena.

When Luxos finished his poem, there was complete silence. Aristophanes held his breath, his fists clenched so tightly his fingernails dug into his palms. He expected the worst. Suddenly the whole theatre erupted into tremendous applause. The shock of hearing such a beautiful poem about the Goddess Athena, from the lips of young Luxos the oarsman's son, had temporarily stunned the audience, but as they regained their voice, there was one of the loudest cheers ever heard in the theatre.

The Goddess Athena

The Goddess Athena did not always watch the comedies at the Dionysia. They were not particularly to her taste. However, on this occasion she was observing, knowing the importance of the event. So it was that she saw Luxos on stage, and heard his poem. She watched the Athenian crowd applaud him and cheer so loudly for an encore that Luxos was obliged to recite it again. After that, he waved to the audience before retreating backstage and slumping to the floor, worn out by the stress of the occasion. Luxos had craved an audience, but he hadn't expected his first performance to be in front of more than twelve thousand inebriated Athenians. He was thrilled that his poem had been so well received, but at the moment his legs had turned to jelly and it would be some time before he could walk again.

Aristophanes

Aristophanes had hardly recovered from the shock of Luxos's triumph when the strange foreign woman, Bremusa, ran into the backstage area carrying a huge box. A scenery painter who got in her way was sent sprawling. She walked swiftly towards Aristophanes and dumped the box at his feet.

'We rescued your phalluses.'

Aristophanes could have jumped for joy, and might have, had time not been so short. As it was he wrenched open the box and screamed at all the stagehands and dressers who were milling around.

'Strap these penises on the chorus and get them out there before there's a riot!'

Overcome with gratitude, he grabbed hold of Bremusa and embraced her. Her body went rigid in shock.

'Thank you for bringing them back.'

The Athenian stagehands could work quickly in a crisis. It took very little time to get the phalluses strapped on. The audience were still in a good mood following Luxos's poem to Athena when the chorus emerged onto the stage. They went into their opening dance, huge phalluses flopping and flying in every direction. The audience cheered. Applause rang round the auditorium. It was a better start than could have been hoped for only a few minutes before.

Aristophanes noticed Luxos lying on the floor, his face still pale.

'Thank you, Luxos.'

'That was very stressful,' mumbled Luxos.

'The Athenian theatre is grateful for your efforts. The muses will reward you generously.'

The Play

Philippus, wearing the comic mask of the lead character, Trygaeus the farmer, had mounted the giant beetle. Lifted by the stage crane, he flew over the heads of the audience.

'I'm off to heaven to visit the gods! I'll find out why they'd abandoned us!'

On stage below, his daughter looked up in alarm.

'My father's gone mad!'

Trygaeus used his phallus as a rudder, steering the beetle from one side of the arena to the other. Below him, the audience howled with laughter.

'Mad?' he cried. 'I'm the only sane person in Athens!'

Kleonike

It was rather beneath the dignity of a priestess to directly involve herself in bribery. Kleonike felt it was impious of Euphranor even to ask her. On the other hand, it did involve being paid a healthy commission. The upkeep of her temple required money, and that had been in short supply recently.

You could say that I was doing my religious duty, bringing in much-needed drachmas, thought Kleonike.

She intercepted Mnesarete on her way into the theatre. Mnesarete was a pretty young girl. Kleonike could see that she might well impress the judges if she walked onstage naked, as apparently she was intended to do.

'Mnesarete. About your appearance at the end of the play.'

'Yes?'

Kleonike produced a bag of silver coins, and showed her one of them, a bright, new tetradrachm.

'What if a sudden unfortunate headache made you unable to appear?'

Mnesarete looked at the gleaming coin, and then at the bag.

'Now you mention it,' she said. 'I am feeling rather unwell.'

She held out her hand. Kleonike gave her the bag of coins.

'I should probably go home and rest,' said Mnesarete.

The Play

Trygaeus flew to heaven and dismounted from the beetle. In heaven – which was of course the same wooden stage he'd taken off from a few minutes before – he was surprised to find there was no one there. All the gods and goddesses seemed to have departed. Only Hermes remained.

The actor playing Hermes, in a mask less comic and more dignified than those worn by the other performers, looked imperiously down at Trygaeus as he approached. Meanwhile the chorus moved smoothly into position, ready to assist in the conversation.

'You shameless villain!' cried Hermes. 'How dare you invade heaven on a giant dung beetle.'

'I'm not a villain! I'm Trygaeus of Athmonon in Athens, an honest farmer. I've brought you a present!'

Trygaeus pulled some meat from his bag and offered it to Hermes, who wolfed it down rather quickly. His hostility towards his visitor visibly lessened.

'I'm here to talk to Zeus,' said the farmer. 'Is he around?'

'Is he around? You've come looking for Zeus? Ha! You've wasted your time. The gods all packed up and left.'

'Why?'

'Because they're sick of you,' replied Hermes, imperiously. 'Sick of you Athenians, and Spartans, and all the other Greeks fighting all the time. They moved out, and they left War behind to do whatever he wants with you.

'And can you blame them?' he continued, declaiming loudly as he turned to face the audience. 'Every time they gave your cities an opportunity for peace, you rejected it. If the Spartans got an advantage in battle, they'd clamour for the war to continue so they could make the Athenians pay. If the Athenians got an advantage, they did exactly the same thing. Both cities could have ended the war any time in the past decade but you were all too stubborn.'

The audience were responding well. Laughter rolled around the amphitheatre and for the first time a festive atmosphere could be felt in the warmth of the late afternoon.

Not everyone in the audience was happy. General Lamachus, seated with other notable citizens, was scowling silently. In the less prestigious seats, Hyperbolus and Euphranor were looking annoyed.

'I don't like the way the audience is lapping this up,' said the weapon-maker.

'Don't worry,' growled Hyperbolus. 'There are still some surprises to come.'

On the low wooden stage, Trygaeus was still engaged in conversation with the god Hermes.

'Surely the Goddess of Peace hasn't completely abandoned us?'

'Peace?' said Hermes. 'War took her and threw her in a cave. You'll never see her again.'

The chorus sighed, lamenting for Greece, and singing of her continuing misfortune. Watching from the wings, Aristophanes allowed himself a tiny ray of optimism. They'd had a rocky start, but the play was now going well.

'Wait till the audience sees our giant statue,' whispered Hermogenes. 'It's going to be great.'

The rescue of the Goddess of Peace, in the form of their new

149

statue, had gone brilliantly in rehearsal. The statue was so splendid, so noble, so colourful, so fitting for the Goddess of Peace in every way, that the sight of it being brought up from the underground cavern couldn't fail to impress the audience. It would rise through the trapdoor as a magnificent symbol of the possibility of ending the war and restoring Athens to its former state of peace and prosperity.

At the centre of the stage Trygaeus was going about the business of rescuing Peace. He'd gathered together the men of the chorus, now representing the honest farmers and artisans of Athens. A rope had been lowered into the trapdoor.

'Citizens of Greece, if we're going to rescue Peace we need everyone to pull together – stop laughing at the back – get these weapon-makers and politicians out the way, we only need farmers and honest citizens here. Everyone ready? Pull!'

There was great straining and effort as they attempted to rescue Peace. The trapdoor opened slowly. The audience held their breath.

'Here she comes!' cried Trygaeus. 'We've rescued the great Goddess of Peace!'

Peace emerged. Unfortunately, it was not the magnificent new statue as paid for by Aristophanes. It was instead the tiny, ragged doll they'd been using in rehearsal. It rose on the end of the rope, a pathetic sight, and one quite baffling for the audience. Trygaeus, caught unawares, looked at it, completely nonplussed. The chorus shifted uncomfortably, not knowing what had gone wrong.

In the stalls, Hyperbolus and Euphranor roared with laughter and took the opportunity to start booing again, their catcalls being taken up by their allies in the audience.

'Booooo! Booooo!'

'We hate your pathetic statue!'

'Aristophanes is making fools of us.'

In the wings, Aristophanes and Hermogenes were open-mouthed with horror.

'Hyperbolus and his cronies have switched our statues!'

'It's a disaster,' wailed Aristophanes.

Trygaeus was an experienced actor, and used to things going wrong. Even so, this was a severe blow and one that was difficult to cope with. He did his best.

'Eh ... you see, fellow Greeks, by our combined efforts we have rescued the great Goddess of Peace – or rather this small but nonetheless impressive representation of her – but the eh ... important point is, we all worked together and—'

The audience were not so easily pacified.

'Booooo! It's the worst prop ever! They're too cheap to spend any money! Booooo!'

Aristophanes

Aristophanes sprinted down the stairs to the room beneath the trapdoor. He cursed his naivety in not posting a guard there, but really, the Dionysia was meant to be a sacred occasion. He hadn't been expecting his enemies to stoop so low as to interfere with his props.

They must have bribed the attendants to let them in, so they could send up the doll to humiliate me. If I don't do something quickly we're doomed.

The actors onstage had been thrown badly off their stride. The play was grinding to a halt and the audience were starting to jeer. At the foot of the stairs Aristophanes ran into Bremusa. It gave him a sudden inspiration.

'I need you to pretend to be the Goddess of Peace!'

'What?'

Above them they could hear Trygaeus fumbling for words. It wasn't going that well.

'I have to send something life-size up there. Get on the platform!'

'Why me?' said Bremusa.

'You're the only woman in the vicinity!'

'I'm not doing it.'

'You have to! If you don't the play will fail!'

Bremusa glared at him. Aristophanes caught her on a weak point. She had been instructed by the goddess to help him. Aristophanes bundled her onto the platform and yanked the rope.

'Take her up!' he cried, then sprinted back to the stairs. He was gasping for breath by the time he made it back to the wings. Fruit and vegetables were again raining down but Philippus, despite his faults, was a plucky performer, one who'd faced an angry audience before. He stood his ground, and improvised as best as he could.

'I'm sure, citizens, that the real goddess we're just about to rescue will be a stupendous creature . . . Look! The cave is opening again! Here is our beautiful Goddess of Peace!'

The trapdoor opened and up came Bremusa, Amazon warrior, with a scowl on her face, a sword in her hand, and a dagger in her belt.

'What?' said Hermogenes, and looked very doubtful. Aristophanes, however, had a feeling that this would go well. The audience were silent for a moment. There were a few comments from the front rows.

'I must say, she's very life-like.'

'Where did they get that costume? It must be eight hundred years old.'

'Why is the Goddess of Peace carrying so many weapons?'

'Is it meant to be satirical?'

'I think it's funny.'

It was funny. As the Goddess of Peace, in armour, with a sword in her hand, scowled out at the audience, looking like she might cleave anyone in two if they annoyed her, the audience began to laugh. The absurdity of it fitted the tone of the play, so much so that Aristophanes wondered if it might have been a better idea to go in that direction from the beginning.

He turned to Hermogenes. 'We're getting away with it ... for Zeus's sake, get the play moving before we lose the audience again. Is Mnesarete ready to go on?'

'She's disappeared.'

'What?'

'She's gone. I think someone might have bribed her to leave.'

Aristophanes glared at Hermogenes. 'Do you have to give me bad news every time you open your mouth? What sort of assistant are you?'

'It's not my fault.'

'Of course it's your fault. You're my assistant! You should have known that Hyperbolus and his cronies might bribe Mnesarete. Unlikely though it may have seemed at the time. What are we going to do now? '

Aristophanes cursed, very loudly. What was the world coming to if you couldn't trust a prostitute?

Luxos

Muses, daughters of Zeus, let us hymn the blessed ones with immortal songs.

Luxos the Poet lay on the ground, happy but drained. Metris the nymph was kneeling beside him. She put her face close to his.

'Your poem was so good! The audience loved you.'

'I feel weak,' mumbled Luxos.

'I'll make you better,' said Metris. She kissed him. Luxos felt strength returning to his limbs.

'Won't this make Athena angry again?' he said.

'How could she mind, after your beautiful poem?'

They kissed again, quite oblivious to the whirlwind of theatrical activity happening all around, as characters rushed on and off stage, and props were carried here and there. Onstage, the chorus was going through one of their dance routines, and the audience were cheering and clapping along.

Aristophanes

With Mnesarete treacherously departed – Aristophanes would have some strong words to say to Theodota about that – they needed a beautiful young woman quickly. That was a problem.

'Find someone beautiful!' he yelled.

'Like who?' said Hermogenes. 'We didn't bring an extra supply.'

Aristophanes fretted. What could he do? Who could he send on? Bremusa? He shook his head. She was an attractive woman but fierce, and not suitable to offer as a bribe to the judges. Besides, his whole strategy was to send out someone practically naked, and he knew she wouldn't do that. Aristophanes had never seen her in anything but her leather armour. He was briefly distracted by the thought of what she might look like without it. He shook his head. No time for that at the moment.

He could send on a man in a female mask and costume. That was standard practice for any speaking role, as there were no female actresses. Some of their young actors made not a bad job of acting the female parts. But it wasn't going to be enough for what he had in mind.

He noticed Luxos and Metris, embracing on the floor. Aristophanes studied the nymph. There was no denying that she was a gorgeous young creature. *Too gorgeous to be kissing Luxos,* he thought, even though he was feeling more sympathetic to the young wretch, after his poetry had saved the day.

Aristophanes was still amazed that he'd turned out to have talent. Not only had his hymn to Athena been a beautiful piece, he'd declaimed it perfectly, and his lyre music had been excellent.

He stepped up and addressed the couple, raising his voice above the commotion in the theatre. 'Young lady, kindly stop kissing that malcontent and listen closely. I need someone shapely and attractive to get out there and shake herself at the judges. You'll just about do. Also, you have to be nearly naked.'

Metris looked up from the floor. 'How naked exactly?'

'As close as we can get without breaking festival law.'

'What does that mean?'

'We'll give you a piece of string.'

She sat up, as did Luxos.

'Why should I do that?'

'To help my play.'

Metris didn't look all that interested in helping his play.

'I'll pay you well.'

That did seem to make more of an impression. There was a pause as she considered it. The chorus was coming to the end of their song. They needed someone onstage soon.

'Are you going to let Luxos have the poetry spot before your play at the next festival?' asked Metris.

'No,' said Aristophanes.

'Then I'm not doing it.'

The chorus were finishing. Aristophanes needed this woman onstage right now, damn her. 'All right! If I win the prize, I'll let him recite again!' He turned to Hermogenes. 'Bring the tiny costume.'

'It's all right,' said Metris, springing to her feet. She smiled broadly. She had a dazzling smile. 'I don't need your costume.'

She stepped behind a wooden pillar. A few seconds later, she stepped out again. How she did what she did, no one could tell, but they had rarely seen such a sight. Her clothes had vanished and she was dressed in a costume which amounted to no more than nine or ten daisies, strategically placed, and attached by some magical means known only to nymphs. While wearing only a few flowers, she'd also caused her hair to be filled with them, so that it rose and spilled over her shoulders in a great wave of buttercups and daisies. Aristophanes gazed at her, astonished at the transformation. So did Hermogenes, and everyone else backstage. It really seemed as if some festive goddess had decided to pay them a visit. No one had ever seen anyone more beautiful. Not only was she beautiful, she seemed to project an aura that spread warmth and happiness around her. Previously stressed stagehands began to smile. Her beauty and warmth produced an overwhelming eroticism – so overwhelming that Aristophanes was obliged to shake his head vigorously to remind himself that they still had a play to finish.

Philippus appeared, waiting for his cue to go back onstage.

'What's happening—' he began, but halted at the sight of Metris. He looked at her in wonder.

'Take her onstage,' yelled Aristophanes. 'And get her as close to the judges as you can.'

Philippus, a solid professional, swiftly overcame his surprise and led Metris out onto the stage. As she walked past the chorus, their phalluses shot in the air, comically erect. The crowd cheered wildly.

'They're huge!'

'Best phalluses ever!'

Aristophanes smiled. He had a shrewd idea that it wasn't just the comedy penises of the chorus that had suddenly gone erect. Metris, clad in only a few daisies, was quite a sight. It was difficult not to react. If Dionysus was looking down on the festival, he surely would have approved.

Trygaeus led Metris around the stage. There was terrific applause from the audience. The nymph smiled at everyone. The warmth of her smile permeated the amphitheatre, and if felt like they were all touched by the cheerful, intoxicated sexual desire that was appropriate at the Dionysia, but had been missing so far. For someone who'd never been on stage before, Metris knew how to milk the applause. She and Trygaeus deliberately took a long time before finally coming to a halt in front of the judges. These judges, five in number, were seated in a prominent position in the front row. They were just as affected by Metris as everyone else, leaning forward in their seats with lustful expressions quite surprising for some of them, given their age.

'Esteemed panel of judges,' said Philippus, declaiming grandly. 'You see what I'm offering you?'

He looked towards Metris, and grinned. 'You get plenty of good things when you award Aristophanes the prize! Athens gets peace, the farmers get their vineyards back, and we all retire for some feasting and debauchery!'

That went down well with the crowd. They all liked feasting and debauchery.

Apart from Socrates, I suppose, thought Aristophanes. *Maybe Euripides too.*

'Hey,' said Luxos, appearing at his elbow. 'What's the idea of offering Metris to the judges? She's not a prostitute.'

'It's just part of the play, you idiot. He's not really offering her. It's metaphorical. How did you end up with such a beautiful girl anyway? You're the city's most notorious layabout. By the way, thanks for reciting your poem at the start.'

'And saving the day?'

'Possibly. I expect my play would have triumphed anyway.'

The chorus, also fans of feasting and debauchery, were doing one of their choreographed happy dances. The audience were cheering and clapping along. The third actor onstage, taking on the personality of a weapons manufacturer, wrung his hands in misery at the prospect of peace.

'My weapons factory!' he wailed. 'I'll be ruined!'

The musicians played as the chorus danced. Metris moved in time with the rhythm. The sight of this produced further roars of approval. The scene had now become so riotous, with the crowd baying, the chorus dancing, the judges laughing and smiling, that it took Trygaeus a while to calm everyone down enough for him to make himself heard.

> *I've saved all of Greece*
> *From the north to the south*
> *By finally shutting*
> *Hyperbolus's mouth!*

Aristophanes looked over to Hyperbolus in the audience. He was furious, naturally, but he controlled his temper, even as some of his opponents poured scorn on him. It was not the done thing to show anger or offer violence in the theatre. If you were ridiculed from the stage, you just had to take it, in public at least. Aristophanes knew there might be trouble ahead. Hyperbolus might follow Kleon's example and prosecute him in court. For now, he didn't care. He knew how well his play had been received. *Peace* had gone down far better than Leucon's *The Clansmen* or Eupolis's *The Flatterers*. As the sun began to sink over the acropolis above, the audience were cheering the final scenes, where Trygaeus was marrying Metris in a symbolic celebration of peace, surrounded by a happy crowd of revellers. Even Bremusa looked happy, something Aristophanes had never seen before. He thought she had a pleasant smile, when she wasn't looking fierce.

The Amphitheatre

Torches were lit as dusk arrived. The audience were laughing and joking as they made their way from the amphitheatre. Friends called to each other, repeating their favourite lines from the day's comedies.

'Do you feel that?' said Nicias to Socrates, near the exit. 'Aristophanes' comedy has changed the whole atmosphere. It's like a weight has lifted from the city. Even our Spartan guests look cheerful. You know, I think we're going to make peace!'

Nicias and the Spartan General Antimachus bowed politely to each other. They were heading for the conference room at the north of the building, pressed into service as the location for the last session of the peace conference. The other Spartan delegates were close behind, and various important Athenians, scattered throughout the theatre, also began to make their way to the conference room.

At the same time, five more Athenians, randomly chosen as judges, were entering the smaller conference room. There they'd deliberate on the comedies they'd seen, and place them first, second and third. Most of the departing audience assumed that Aristophanes would win. His play hadn't gone perfectly, but it had certainly made them laugh the most. The girl at the end had been spectacular. She was a topic of conversation in the city for many weeks afterwards.

> *I would much prefer to see*
> *the graceful way she carries herself*
> *and the radiance of her features*
> *than talk of war-chariots or hoplites*
>
> **Sappho**

Aristophanes

After the play, everyone was in high spirits backstage. The lead actors and members of the chorus strutted around, telling each other how good they'd been or, even better, letting other people tell them. The chorus were particularly ecstatic. As amateurs, they weren't used to the stresses involved. Though they'd all tried to hide it during rehearsals, they'd been terrified of the play being a flop, and finding themselves ridiculed by their fellow citizens. The sense of relief they felt was overwhelming, and the wine was flowing freely. A few of their wives had appeared from the audience to share in their celebration. Everyone knew the play had been good, and Aristophanes was roundly congratulated on all sides. Hermogenes' wife wasn't there, though the young man on whom he spent most of his money was. Luxos and Metris were sitting in a corner, staring lovingly at each other.

'Well, Aristophanes, you've done it again,' said Hermogenes. 'Another triumph.'

He was smiling broadly. Aristophanes tried to smile back, but he found it difficult. After the brief elation at the end of the play, he'd started to worry again.

'I hope the judges liked it,' he muttered. 'You can never trust them to get it right.'

The statesman Nicias arrived. 'Aristophanes! I'm on my way to the conference but I just had to call in and congratulate you. What a splendid comedy! You made the warmongers look like fools. You know, it may just have tipped things in our favour!'

Nicias seemed genuinely optimistic. He really thought it might have made a difference. After he departed, Hermogenes' smile grew even broader. 'Even Nicias liked it and he's one of the most important men in the city. This is a great day, Aristophanes.'

'I suppose so.'

Hermogenes frowned. 'What's the matter? You've just had a huge triumph and you don't seem happy.'

'A huge triumph? Only if the judges agree.'

'It's a triumph anyway. The audience loved it. And you heard Nicias. Your play might even help to end the war. How many playwrights can say that?'

Again Aristophanes tried to smile, but he couldn't. He was too worried about the judges.

'Is winning the competition really the only thing you care about?'

'Yes.'

Hermogenes stared at him. 'Sometimes I don't like you very much, Aristophanes. Excuse me.' He departed, back to his favourite youth, and a cup of wine.

Bremusa appeared. 'I was listening to your conversation. Now I think I'm starting to understand culture. It means you have to defeat your opponents, right?'

'It seems to be that way with me,' admitted Aristophanes. 'Others might not agree.'

He handed her some wine. 'Hermogenes thinks it's a flaw in my character.'

'A flaw?' said Bremusa. 'The desire to win? How can that be a flaw?'

Aristophanes remembered the debt he owed Bremusa. 'Thanks for saving me from that assassin. And for rescuing my phalluses. And for being the Goddess of Peace. More wine?'

'When will the judges make their decision?'

'Not for an hour or so. It always takes them a while. Probably because they need time to wolf down as much free food and drink as possible.'

Though Aristophanes' mood had not much improved, it wasn't affecting the celebrations around them, which had now grown. All sorts of people were crowding in, including Socrates and a few of his associates. As Aristophanes looked on, Theodota entered. His heart leapt, and he waited for her to come over and congratulate him. She didn't come over. Instead she made directly for Socrates and draped herself over him like a curtain. Bremusa saw Aristophanes frowning. She followed his gaze.

'Why do you spend so much time and money on a woman who isn't really interested in you?'

'I see that tact isn't your strong point.'

'Tact is for weaklings. Why do you care about her?'

Aristophanes shrugged, hopelessly. 'I'm an artist. We're not very good at relationships. You might say it's another flaw in my character.'

Bremusa laughed. There was a slight touch of battle fury in it, but it wasn't altogether an unpleasant sound. Aristophanes found himself taking to her more. Could she really have fought at Troy? He was still half-convinced she was a madwoman. Though she was good with a sword. Her companion Metris certainly couldn't be from this world. Not with the effect she had on people. She was now doing a slow dance with Luxos in the middle of the room, and the young men looking on were hypnotised.

'I've never been scared in battle,' said Bremusa. 'But when I went onstage I was trembling. I was blinded by stage fright. I hardly even saw the theatre.'

She pursed her lips. 'I think I've missed out. Since I've been in Athens I haven't really seen anything.'

'Would you like to see the theatre now? It's a fine building. If you look up, you can see the Parthenon with the moon shining through the columns.'

Aristophanes led Bremusa back outside. She'd undone the top of her leather armour because of the warmth of the evening. It made her look a little less militaristic. They gazed out at the rows of empty seats. Aristophanes loved the amphitheatre; he loved its circular shape and the happy world he could create there.

'I was only nineteen when I put on my first play.'

Bremusa nodded. He asked her what she'd been doing when she was nineteen.

'Fighting,' she replied, which is what he'd been expecting.

She was standing close. Aristophanes had a sudden urge to take her in his arms. He might have done it, had not a freezing wave swept over the theatre, a shockwave that felt both physical and mental. Aristophanes staggered under the assault. As he regained his balance he saw a figure emerge from the shadows. A woman in dark clothes, with long hair, fine cheekbones and very pale skin. She had a twisted metal emblem hanging from a chain round her neck. Something snake-like, he couldn't quite make it out.

'My name is Laet.'

Given the powerful wave of negative feelings that emanated from her, her voice was rather soft. Laet strode towards them, very erect. She looked Aristophanes directly in the eye. It gave him the uncomfortable feeling that everything in his life had gone wrong, and would never be right again.

'I enjoyed your comedy,' she said. 'Fine poetry. Fine songs. You have a rare command of the language. I laughed. It's a long time since I've laughed at anything.'

She paused. 'So I'm going to give you a choice. I don't usually give people choices.'

Aristophanes was finding it difficult to speak.

'What choice?' asked Bremusa.

'It's time to make decisions. There are two conference rooms here. In one, the judges are discussing which play should win first prize. In the other, it's the last session of the peace conference.'

Laet smiled. 'Whichever room I enter, they'll make a foolish decision.'

Aristophanes didn't like the sound of this, but he was still finding it difficult to speak. Laet's malevolent smile was making it worse.

'Your play was the best,' she continued. 'But if I go into the judges' room, they'll make the wrong choice. You won't win first prize.'

Laet paused for a moment, to let that sink in.

'I could visit the peace conference instead. If I do that, they'll make a bad decision. They won't sign the treaty, and Athens will remain at war.'

She smiled her chilling smile. 'Which room would you like me to enter?'

Aristophanes could still feel the freezing wave of misery, but at last he managed to speak. 'Couldn't you stay out of both?'

Laet's expression hardened. 'I'm entering one of them.'

At that moment Luxos emerged onto the stage, with Metris behind him. The nymph's presence slightly alleviated the chilling aura emanating from Laet, though not by much.

'What's this?' said Luxos. He sounded upset. 'Aristophanes has to win. Otherwise he won't let me recite my poetry at the next festival.'

'That would be a shame,' said Laet. 'You do have some talent.'

'If I don't win I'm going to have a lot of difficulty paying my staff and helpers,' said Aristophanes.

At this, Metris looked unhappy. 'But I was going to use my wages to repair my temple.'

'What's happening out here?' Hermogenes, his boyfriend, and Philippus arrived on the scene. 'Did I hear someone say we're not getting paid? Again?'

Philippus scowled. 'I thought this year I'd finally be in the winning play.'

'Eupolis or Leucon can't win,' said Aristophanes. 'It's just not fair.'

'Nothing is fair these days,' said Laet. 'And you're running out of time.' She turned her head to stare at the wall at the far end of the amphitheatre, as if she could see through to the rooms beyond.

'You have three minutes.'

Laet turned and walked back into the shadows, leaving a confused group of people behind her.

'You have to make peace,' said Hermogenes.

'Eh ... well ...' Aristophanes didn't seem to share Hermogenes' strong views. 'That means I'll lose the competition.'

'Your whole play was about making peace!'

Alone among the gathering, Metris was unaffected by Laet's freezing aura. She followed her into the shadows.

'This isn't very nice of you,' said the nymph.

Laet didn't reply.

'Why are you so mean?'

'Mean? I wouldn't say I was mean. I fulfil a function.'

'Why?'

'I'm already bored by your questions.'

'I wish you hadn't destroyed the Altar of Pity. It was a lovely old altar.'

Laet wore the same cold smile. 'They tried to repair it. And re-sanctify it. The Archon Basileus himself came down to perform the ceremony. For all the good it did.'

Metris nodded sadly. 'They can't make it the way it was. You're too powerful.'

'I know. And I'm too powerful for you, nymph, even if you can warm a few hearts.'

Metris nodded again. It was true. Laet was too powerful.

'I tried making buttercups and daises to help the altar. But I couldn't make any grow.'

Laet nodded. 'That was a futile effort. Though actually, it wasn't me that prevented you.'

'Wasn't it?'

'No. Your power here is waning. All the power of the immortals is waning in Athens. The gods are withdrawing.'

'Why?'

'It's just time for it to happen.' Laet's eyes narrowed. 'I'll spread some misery before I go.'

'Did something really horrible happen to you when you were young?' asked Metris. 'So it left you hating everyone?'

A furious expression flickered over Laet's face. She controlled it quickly. 'My past is no concern of yours. It's time for Aristophanes to make his decision.'

She strode back towards the stage.

'Well?' she demanded.

Everyone looked towards Aristophanes. He turned to

Bremusa, hoping for some help, but while Bremusa seemed quite calm, she had no advice for him. He could choose either to win the play competition, or win peace for Athens.

'Zeus damn it,' he muttered. 'We can't risk the peace conference failing. I suppose you'd better go into the judges' room.'

Laet nodded.

'Wait,' called Aristophanes.

'Yes?'

'If we make peace now, will Athens return to her former prosperity?'

'I'm not an oracle. The oracles are coming to an end. Am I the only one who realises that?'

She walked off. Aristophanes turned to Bremusa. 'Can't you kill her or something?'

'No. I'm not allowed. Sorry.'

Socrates emerged from the wings. Theodota followed. Athens' most beautiful and wealthy hetaera trailing around after Athens' ugliest philosopher. Aristophanes scowled. He'd never understand it.

'What just happened?' asked Socrates.

'Athens made peace.'

'Oh. That's good. Why does no one look happy?'

Bremusa took Aristophanes' hand. 'It's all right,' she said. 'You still triumphed. Everyone saw it. You don't need the prize.'

Aristophanes' strength deserted him. He sat down on the edge of the stage.

'Triumph,' he mumbled. 'Ha.'

Pindar

When toils have been resolved, festivity is the best
physician;

Songs, the skilful daughters of the Muses, soothe with
    their touch
Words of praise married to the music of the lyre
Will comfort more than the hot spring.
Words live longer than deeds
When, by the Graces' assent,
They rise up out of the deep heart.

Bremusa

Next day, Bremusa watched as a crowd of Athenians made their way to the assembly on Pnyx hill. She hurried towards the agora, now nearly empty. Close to the Altar of the Twelve Gods she concealed herself behind a large statue of a discus thrower. As she crouched there, hidden from sight, she noticed how deftly the sculptor had reproduced the lines of the athlete's calf muscles. For the first time, she felt some appreciation of the sculptor's art.

That must take a lot of skill.

She peered between the statue's legs as Idomeneus came into view, striding into the market, his great black beard marking him out as an ancient warrior, the sword on his back catching the rays of the sun. Bremusa had known he'd buy supplies for Laet, before they left the city. She couldn't let him leave Athens without challenging him. Her honour would not allow it. Yet she knew she couldn't defeat him in face to face combat.

Laet's work was done. Bremusa wondered if the people who'd brought her here were pleased with the results. She doubted that Laet would care; she'd amused herself for a while.

As Idomeneus came near, two children suddenly dashed into his path. Young Plato and Xenophon, rolling a wooden hoop along the ground. They shouted and laughed, absorbed in their game. So absorbed were they that they failed to notice Idomeneus, or so it seemed. They crashed into him, the eight-year-old and nine-year-old hitting one leg each and making the Cretan warrior stagger, just for a second.

Bremusa emerged from her hiding place and leapt towards him. She'd hired the children to distract him and they'd done it admirably. Before Idomeneus knew what was happening, she'd grabbed him from behind and had her knife at his throat, touching the skin.

'Move and I'll kill you,' she said.

'What is this?'

'This is me defeating you in combat. I could kill you now.'

'You think jumping out from behind and putting a knife at my throat is defeating me in combat?'

'Yes.'

Bremusa had a firm grip of Idomeneus's tunic. He couldn't turn round, or move at all, without her knife slitting his throat.

'I never knew an Amazon to act so dishonourably.'

'I just learned some strategy, Idomeneus. Like the Greeks at Troy. And now, by letting you live, my defeat is avenged, and my honour is restored.'

Bremusa released him. Perhaps Idomeneus would have drawn his sword to fight, but they were interrupted by a low-pitched laugh.

'Well, Idomeneus. She did seem to best you. For a moment, anyway.' Laet held out her hand. A stallholder hurried over and placed some grapes in her palm. She put one in her mouth.

'I never expected my visit to Athens to be so entertaining,' she said. 'But we must be off. I'm being paid to curse Melos, and I have something very bad in mind for them.'

Laet wrinkled her nose. 'These children, they do give me a headache. Come, Idomeneus.'

Idomeneus glared at Bremusa with loathing, but followed his mistress out of the agora. Nearby, a stallholder was looking confused, wondering why she'd just given away free grapes to a women she didn't know.

Xenophon and Plato were looking on. They'd done their task well. The Amazon thanked them, awkwardly. She rarely knew what to say to children. 'What are you going to be when you grow up?'

'A warrior,' said Plato.

'A philosopher,' said Xenophon.

'I wish you luck.' Bremusa handed over the silver she'd promised. They ran off, rolling their wooden hoop in front of them.

The Assembly

Nicias was in fine form as he addressed the crowd, speaking much less hesitantly than he normally did. He had good news. It was already known to everyone there, but that didn't take away from Nicias's glory in being the one to announce it.

'... and I hereby confirm that the peace treaty has been signed by myself, Nicias, along with the rest of our delegation, those signatories being Lampon, Isthmonicus, Laches, Euthydemus, Pythodorus, Hagnon, Myrtilus, Lamachus ... '

The crowd listened attentively. The oppressive heat that hung over the city had vanished overnight. Spring had resumed and the mood was positive. The war was finally ending. There were only a few glum faces in the crowd. Hyperbolus was one, and Euphranor another. Then there was Aristophanes, who seemed not to be paying attention at all. He sat with his eyes fixed on the ground, apparently unhappy, despite the good news.

'... the signatories from Sparta being Damagetus, Chionis, Metagenes, Acanthus, Daithus, Ischagoras ...' continued Nicias.

When he'd finished reading out the list of names, he paused, then raised one hand as he spoke to the assembly.

'The war has now ended!'

The cheering was loud and prolonged as the Athenians contemplated the joys of returning to their normal lives. Those farmers who'd been shut behind the city walls for safety were particularly loud in their applause. Now they could return to their farms. Fields would be tilled, vines and figs planted, and goats sent out to pasture.

Oh sweet peace, wealth-giver to mortals

Aristophanes stared at his feet. He barely heard the cheering. He couldn't believe that he'd been cheated out of first prize again.

The Trident

Polykarpos, landlord of the Trident, had rarely seen trade pick up so quickly. There was a mass of business waiting to be done in Athens. As soon as peace was declared, farms, mines and workshops all across the city-state hurried to restart their business. The port was bustling again, and fishing boats were already heading out to sea. Farmers, on their way to market to buy seeds, stopped in at the tavern for a swift drink, meeting friends whose business mending fishing nets was suddenly active again. Potters were busy at their wheels and blacksmiths were hammering out ploughshares, earning money, calling in to the tavern for a reviving drink between shifts. The prostitutes, back in business again, looked much happier, and there were raucous conversations between them and the market women who suddenly had goods to sell.

In the agora they were joking that Hyperbolus and Aristophanes were the only two unhappy men in Athens.

A plague on them anyway, thought Polykarpos. *I've got no time for politicians. Or artists.*

Laet

'That was all a waste of time.' Idomeneus had been in a poor temper ever since they'd left Athens. It wasn't helped by carrying their baggage up the steep hills on their journey north.

'I wouldn't say that, Idomeneus. I was well paid.'

'But Athens made peace, didn't they?'

Laet smiled. 'I repeat, I was well paid. I provide an excellent service, but I offer no guarantees. Why do you care that they made peace, anyway?'

'I hate Athens. I'd rather see them swept away.'

'Really? I didn't dislike them too much. Some of them anyway. Socrates for one. And young Luxos, if only because I wish someone had written a poem like that about me. I wonder what life has in store for him now he's become entangled with the immortals? He may find it stranger than he imagined.'

'To Hades with them all,' grunted Idomeneus.

'Idomeneus, you are tiresome when you're in a bad mood. Don't worry about Athens. My spirit will linger there. They'll make plenty of bad decisions in future. Disastrous decisions, very likely.'

Laet looked west. 'Have you ever been in Syracuse?'

'Syracuse? Why would we go all the way there?'

'Just a notion. I've always enjoyed travelling.'

Luxos

*Muses, daughters of Zeus, let us hymn the blessed ones
with immortal songs.*

At Theodota's house, Luxos was in fine voice, declaiming grandly. He had, it was agreed, a very fine voice for someone of such slender stature. His lyre playing was excellent. The more discerning among his audience could tell that his instrument wasn't the best, and showed obvious signs of recent repair, but he could play it well, and he got a good tone. If he did make one or two fancy flourishes that purists might not like, well, he was young, and they could make allowances.

Luxos stood at one end of the room, beside a splendid statue of a nymph, sculpted by Phidias. It was one of the few pieces by the famous sculptor to be found in private hands. Theodota had never actually confirmed that Phidias had given it to her just before he passed away, nine years ago, for services rendered when she was fifteen, but it was commonly supposed to be the case.

Theodota sat on a gilded chair, listening appreciatively to Luxos. She'd heard all of Greece's most famous poets. Many of them had obliged her with private readings. She'd declared Luxos to be a very talented young man, and his reputation, already high after his performance at the theatre, had risen even further. Beside Theodota were several other elegant courtesans, and behind them their servants. Metris was perched on a table, swinging her legs, and the nymph's presence brought an added cheer to the room.

As Luxos finished his poem, there were smiles and applause. Various women, including Mnesarete, headed straight for him, but they were beaten there by Metris, who did not intend sharing him for the moment.

Aristophanes had complained to Theodota about Mnesarete's treachery, but the hetaera had laughed it off. 'Treachery and bribery are mainstays of Athenian politics,' she'd told him. 'The assembly sets a very bad example. You can't blame my maid if she decided to join in.'

Metris

In the middle of the night, Luxos and Bremusa, appearing from different directions, were greeted by Metris at the edge of the agora.

'Hello! I've asked you both here for a reason. Not that I need a reason, of course. It's always lovely to see you.'

Bremusa was more sympathetic towards Metris now their mission was concluded, but regarded her suspiciously out of habit. Aristophanes had invited the Amazon to visit him; she wondered if the nymph knew that.

'Why are we here?'

Metris pointed towards an ancient piece of stone.

'The Altar of Pity. Laet ruined it. Stonemasons repaired it, and the head of all religion in Athens came to consecrate it. But it isn't working properly.' Her face fell. 'They couldn't really fix it. Laet was too powerful.'

She laid her hand on the altar and sighed. 'No one can pray here properly any more. It's such a shame.'

Bremusa was puzzled. 'Is it really that important? Athens is full of temples. You can hardly move without finding somewhere to pray.'

'This is the Altar of Pity,' said Metris. 'The place of last resort. When everything else fails, you can come here. I thought it was a nice thing to have.'

'I suppose so.'

Luxos liked the altar too. He'd known family members use it, back when he had a family.

'I tried to make it better,' continued Metris. 'But I couldn't. So I asked Goddess Athena if she could help. She couldn't either. She said the altar was older than her, and she had no power over it.'

'Then what do you have in mind?'

'Athena suggested I gather up people with spiritual power and try again.'

Bremusa raised her eyebrows. 'Is that meant to include me? My spiritual power would be around zero, I imagine.'

'I'm sure it's not,' said Metris. 'You've been an Amazon for hundreds of years and you've lived on Mount Olympus. You must have something inside you or that wouldn't have happened. And Luxos, I'm sure you're spiritual. You write such lovely poems.'

Luxos shook his head. 'I'm not that good a poet. And I'm too young. You need to be old and experienced before you can write anything that powerful.'

'We have to try. Don't you know anything that would be appropriate?'

Luxos, for once, looked uncertain on the subject of poetry.

'Isn't there some hymn to Mother Earth, oldest of beings?' said Bremusa.

'Yes, I know that.'

'I'm sure that will be perfect,' said Metris. 'Everyone put your hands on the altar while Luxos recites the poem.'

Beautiful Earth, mother of all, eldest of all beings.
Who sustains all creatures
All that walk upon the bountiful land,
All that are in the seas,
And all that fly.
Through you, O queen, we are blessed in our children
And blessed in our harvests,
Happy is the man whom you delight to honour!

His land is covered with corn, his pastures are full of
    cattle,
His daughters skip merrily over the soft flowers of the
    field.
Thus is it with those whom you honour, O holy goddess.
Hail, Mother of the gods, wife of starry Heaven.

Luxos and Bremusa felt a great warmth spreading from Metris's hands, through theirs, and into the altar. Metris looked down. At the foot of the altar were one buttercup and one daisy. She nodded and smiled. Not her normal, whole-hearted smile, but something more thoughtful.

'That's a little better. We haven't fully repaired it, but it's better. It might still work. Anyone coming here as a last resort might still find help.'

Aristophanes

Aristophanes was suffering from insomnia. He hadn't slept properly since the last night of the Dionysia. The crushing gloom may have lifted from the city but it still afflicted the playwright. He thought of the Spartans, riding home with news that they'd signed the treaty. He wondered if they'd be pleased. Most of them would be, he supposed. Even Spartans didn't like to fight all the time. Most of Athens was certainly pleased. Hyperbolus and his cronies were defeated for the moment, and keeping a low profile in the face of public mockery. Even their discomfiture didn't bring Aristophanes any pleasure. He hadn't won the competition. He'd been awarded second place. Just like last year, when his play *Wasps* had been placed second, even though it was clearly the best comedy at the festival.

He couldn't believe it had happened again. *Peace* had been

175

placed second. Eupolis had won, with a play which was inferior to his in every way.

Aristophanes sighed loudly. He felt dull, fatigued, yet still unable to sleep. He paced around the room, then looked out of the window at the dark streets. He saw a line of torches passing by. A procession, coming from a symposium somewhere. There had been a lot of drinking parties in the past few days. Aristophanes had refused all invitations. Hermogenes was no longer speaking to him. He didn't care. He was sick of the whole city.

Aristophanes knew he wasn't being entirely rational. The city had made peace. His play had been instrumental in that. There was good reason for rejoicing.

But why was I the only one who had to suffer? It simply isn't fair.

He sat down. His eyelids were drooping. He rested his head on his hand and gazed at the table in front of him. There were scrolls there, all blank. Normally he wrote every day, but since the Dionysia he'd been unable to compose a word.

Weariness began to overwhelm him. He experienced a brief, dreamlike feeling, and suddenly the Goddess Athena was standing in front of him. She looked just like Phidias's great statue of her in the Parthenon, with her robe cascading in folds, her bronze helmet pushed back on her head, and a spear in her hand. Aristophanes froze, incapable of movement. He was scared, though she didn't seem hostile. Fortunately, he hadn't insulted her in any of his plays.

The goddess regarded him calmly. 'Aristophanes. It's time for you to cheer up.'

That was more prosaic than he was expecting. If the Goddess Athena ever chose to appear to him, he hadn't thought it would be to tell him to cheer up.

'So you lost to Eupolis,' she continued. 'What of it? You helped bring peace to Greece.'

Aristophanes' fear had receded a little, helped by the goddess's conversational tone. He managed to utter a few words. 'I know. Peace is good. But ... '

'But you can't stand that you lost? Really, Aristophanes, you shouldn't worry about it. Eupolis's play will be forgotten in a few years. So will Leucon's. Your play won't be. Two thousand years in the future, people will still be reading *Peace*.'

Aristophanes was startled. 'Two thousand years? Really?'

'Yes. When every other Athenian comic dramatist has long been forgotten, your name will still be remembered. Your plays will be published in languages that haven't even been invented yet.'

Aristophanes was staring somewhere around the goddess's midriff, not wanting to look her in the eyes, which might be disrespectful, and dangerous. He was moved to glance upwards at the phrase languages that haven't even been invented yet. He liked that.

'Your plays will survive through thousands of years, and be read by people in nations that don't yet exist. They'll be staged in a future you can hardly imagine. People will be applauding Trygaeus on his flying beetle when Eupolis is no more than a footnote in a history book.'

Aristophanes was still struggling to speak. The Goddess Athena didn't seem to mind. He supposed she would be used to it.

'Does this make you feel better?' she asked.

'Much better, Goddess.'

'Good. Now I suggest you brighten up, sleep properly, then start writing your next comedy.'

Athena began to fade from sight, but then, as if changing her mind suddenly, she came sharply into focus again.

'Oh, and Aristophanes ... '

'Yes?'

'Send Bremusa back happy, or there will be trouble.'

With that, the Goddess Athena disappeared. Aristophanes' head snapped back and he came fully awake. He leapt from his chair. It had been a startlingly vivid dream. Or vision, perhaps. The Goddess Athena had appeared to him. He hadn't quite arrived back in reality when he noticed Bremusa standing in the doorway.

'I should take this armour off,' she said. 'I've been wearing it since I arrived in Athens. Do you have a bathing room? With hot water?'

'Yes.'

'Take me there. I have two days before I'm due back on Mount Olympus.'

Luxos

Luxos the poet was more used to the city than the countryside, and toiled as he ascended the steeply rising hills. He had to pick his way carefully through several spiky thickets, and scramble over patches of loose shale and scree. He found it arduous, though it was not quite as hard as it might have been; Luxos had a new pair of sandals, of good quality, his first for some years. Aristophanes had paid him for his help. The payment had been surprisingly generous; in the past few days, the playwright's mood had dramatically improved. Luxos also had a commission from Theodota to write an ode to her beauty, and several invitations to symposiums held by well-connected citizens, where he would be paid to read and would probably pick up more commissions. His performance in the theatre, and his Hymn to Athena, had been widely praised. Doors were opening all over the city to Luxos, and he was no longer a figure of fun.

'That's the good thing about Athens,' he said, to a small sparrow which looked down at him from a branch. 'If you show you have talent, you can get a chance.'

He raised his lyre in the direction of the sparrow. 'Would you like to hear a new poem I've been working on about Aphrodite?'

They clothed her with heavenly garments:
on her head was a fine, well-wrought crown of gold,
her earrings were of orichalc and precious gold,
golden necklaces hung over her soft neck and snow-white
breasts,

The sparrow chirped in appreciation.

'It's just a first draft,' explained Luxos. 'I'll have to ask Metris if she can find out anything more about Aphrodite for me. You'd like Metris. She's wonderful. I'm going to see her now.'

Luxos bade the sparrow a cheery farewell and carried on. After some more arduous scrambling, he finally emerged in an area of green woodland, where the slope was much more gentle.

This looks like the place, he thought. *Metris said she'd meet me here.*

There was no sign of the nymph, though he did think he glimpsed a centaur through the trees. Luxos took a few steps forward and suddenly found Metris right in front of him, smiling. He wasn't sure if she'd stepped out from a behind a tree, or just materialised out of thin air.

'Luxos.' Metris threw her arms around him, and they kissed. 'You found me!'

'I followed your directions.'

'Some people can't get here, even with directions.'

She kissed him again.

'It's so good to see you, Lux,' she said, using her pet name for the young poet. She took his hand and led him along a path between the trees. Flowers grew along the edges of the path, the richest, most colourful flowers Luxos had ever seen.

'It's so exciting! My temple's been repaired!'

'Really?'

Metris nodded enthusiastically. 'Workmen arrived saying Hephaistos had sent them because the Goddess Athena asked him to arrange some building work for her. I just moved in with the naiads for a few days and when I came back the temple was all fixed up, it's really lovely! It's better than ever, they've made it so nice and comfy. Look!'

They rounded a corner. Metris's small temple had been completely renovated. More than that, it had been upgraded. Pillars, previously of grey stone, were now gleaming marble, and there was a finely chiselled statue of the Goddess Athena on the portico. Metris waved cheerfully to the statue. Above the door was an inscription.

TEMPLE OF METRIS
(JUNIOR) GODDESS OF BUTTERCUPS AND DAISIES

'Isn't it lovely?' said Metris. Her youthful face lit up as she surveyed her renovated home. 'And they made me a goddess. Well, a junior goddess anyway. I expect you just have to wait a while before you get promoted.'

Inside the temple there were two shrines. The larger, in the middle, featured another statue of Athena.

'So I can talk to her any time I want. Bremusa said they'd be pleased to hear from me whenever I felt like a chat. She was a lot happier the last time I spoke to her.'

At the back of the main room was a smaller shrine, dedicated to the spirit of nymphs everywhere.

'I thought that was a nice gesture,' said Metris. 'It's time we got the recognition we deserve. And look, they took care of all the details.' She opened a cabinet door, revealing several large amphoras full of wine.

'Enough for libations, with plenty left over for me.'

The rear of the temple had been renovated, extended and remodelled into new living quarters. In a very comfortable room, full of quilts and cushions, Luxos and Metris drank a little wine, lay down together and gazed into each other's eyes.

Glossary

Acropolis	An ancient citadel located on a high rocky outcrop above the city of Athens. Site of the Parthenon, the Temple of Athena Nike, and other public buildings. The temples of the Acropolis were destroyed by the Persians in 480 BC, and rebuilt under the leadership of the Athenian statesman Pericles.
Agora	Open space in Greek city, used for both commerce and public meetings. In Athens the agora was surrounded by important buildings, including temples and the law courts.
Amazon	Mythical race of female warriors.
Amphora	Large ceramic jar, commonly used for storing wine.
Athmonon	Attica, the region of Greece ruled by Athens, was divided into administrative units called Demes. Athmonon, a rural area, was one of those demes.
Chiton	Athenian garment. A rectangular piece of linen or wool draped over the wearer, held in place at the shoulders by brooches and at the waist by a belt. Worn knee length by Athenian men, and ankle length by women.
Choregos	A wealthy Athenian citizen who was assigned the task of financing a play at the festival. This was regarded as an honour, though it could be a serious drain on the citizen's resources.
Cottabus	A game played at dinner parties. The objective was to throw the dregs of wine from your drinking cup towards a small statue on top of

a bronze stand. To win, you had to knock the statue off its plinth, making it fall into a container below. Participants reclined on their couches while playing.

Delium	City, north of Athens. Site of the Battle of Delium between the Athenians and the Boeotians, in which Athens was defeated. In Plato's *Symposium*, Alcibiades talks to Aristophanes about Socrates' bravery in the aftermath of this battle.
Delphi	Location of the Delphic Oracle, best-known and most authoritative of the ancient oracles.
Deme	Administrative sub-division of Athens and the surrounding region.
Dionysia	An Important Athenian festival. The book is set in the City Dionysia. (There was also a Rural Dionysia.) It took place in the month of Elaphebolion which today would be March or April.
Drachma	Athenian coin, equal to six obols.
Ephor	Important officials in Sparta, sharing power with the Spartan joint Kings.
Gymnastae	One of the various classes of officials responsible for both the physical and moral training of youths at the gymnasium.
Hesiod	Poet, from Boeotia in central Greece, active round 700 BC and roughly contemporary with Homer. He was highly regarded by the ancient Greeks. Some of his work was mythological in nature but some of it dealt with the harsh realities of life as a farmer.
Hetairai	The highest class of courtesans in Athens. As well their beauty, hetairai were valued as good companions because of their education and

intelligence. They could also be skilled musicians and singers. They were not native Athenian citizens, usually coming from other Greek cities. Unlike most women in Athens at the time, hetairai could legally control their own financial affairs.

Hoplite	Athenian foot soldier. Well-equipped, with bronze armour and bronze-covered shield. They carried a long spear and a sword. Trained to fight in formation, in the phalanx. Luxos would have been too poor to afford his own armour, and probably would have served in the light troops who supported the hoplites.
Krater	Large vessel used for diluting wine with water. Usually ceramic, occasionally made of metal.
Laurium	The silver mines at Laurium, south-east of Athens, were an important source of income for the city-state. The Athenians used the wealth to build up their navy, a major part of their military power. The silver was also used for Athenian coinage, which was valued all over the ancient Greek world.
Lyceum	Named for its Patron Apollo Lyceus (Apollo in the form of a wolf) the Lyceum was originally an open-air meeting place. By the time of Aristophanes there was a gymnasium for wrestling and athletics. The grounds were also used for military training. Later the Lyceum became associated with Aristotle, who founded his school there.
Lysistrata	Comedy, performed in Athens in 411 BC.
Medea	Play by Euripides, produced in Athens in 431 BC. At the end of the play, Medea travels to 'the land of Erechtheus,' meaning Athens.

Melos	The inhabitants of the Island of Melos were virtually wiped out in 415 BC by an Athenian military expedition.
Muse	The Muses were goddesses who provided the inspiration for literature, science and the arts. According to Hesiod's *Theogony*, (7th century BC) there were nine muses, daughters of Zeus and Mnemosyne.
Olympus, Mount	The highest mountain in Greece. In Greek mythology, Mount Olympus was the home of the Gods.
Pandionis	In the 5th century BC, Athenian citizens were organised into ten tribes, of which Pandionis was one. Each tribe contained members from the city itself, and from the surrounding region of Attica. The Pandionis tribe was named after Pandion, a legendary king of Athens.
Parthenon	A temple on the Acropolis, famed in ancient and modern times. The Parthenon was dedicated to the Goddess Athena. It was part of the rebuilding project carried out by Pericles after the destruction caused by the Persian invasion in 480 BC. The Parthenon housed a huge ivory and gold statue of Athena, regarded as one of the wonders of the ancient world, sculpted by Phidias. The Parthenon also served as a treasury.
Piraeus	Port, harbour and shipyard, south-west of Athens, and the base of its powerful fleet. The corridor of land between Athens and Piraeus was enclosed and protected by the Long Walls, constructed by order of Pericles in the mid 5th century BC.
Pnyx	A hill in Athens. Citizens gathered on the Pnyx

	to hold their democratic assemblies.
Salamis	An island about a mile from the coast at Piraeus. In 480 BC, around 60 years before events in this book, the combined navy of the Greek city-states, led by Athens, destroyed the Persian fleet in the narrow strait between Salamis and the mainland. The Persian King, Xerxes, immediately fled. His invading army, which had occupied Athens, was soon annihilated.
Scythian Archers	The Scythian Archers were slaves, owned by the state, who acted as guards or watchmen in Athens, making up some sort of police force. Historians today know very little about them.
Sparta	Greek city-state, Athens' main rival for supremacy in Greece during the 5th century BC. Famed for their military training, the Spartan army was regarded as unbeatable at this time. Athens was the dominant naval force, but they were unable to match Sparta on land, and were forced to withdraw behind their walls when the Spartans ventured into Attica. Shortly before the time of this book, Athens had scored an unexpected victory over a Spartan force at Pylos, and taken Spartan prisoners. These prisoners gave Athens a powerful bargaining chip in negotiations.
Symposiarch	The Symposiarch acted as master of ceremonies at the symposium. His main duty was to regulate drinking. Athenians always diluted their wine with water. (Wine in ancient Greece may have been stronger than it is today.) The symposiarch was responsible for deciding by how much the wine should be

diluted, and how often drinks were passed round. It was bad form for a symposium to descend into a drunken rabble, and the symposiarch was supposed to prevent this from happening. Despite this, it was known to occur.

Symposium
A drinking party. Usually associated with the educated gentlemen of Athens. Activities could vary, from serious philosophical and political discussions, to heavy drinking and carousing with flute-girls.

Tetradrachm
Athenian silver coin, equal to four drachma. Widely used in the ancient Greek world.

Troy
City in Anatolia, now part of modern Turkey. Site of the famous Trojan war, as recounted by Homer. While Homer's epic contains many mythical elements, many modern scholars believe that there was a war between Greeks and Trojans, probably around 1200 BC.

Afterword

I admire the ancient Athenians for many reasons. I like their architecture, their statues, their pottery and their writing. They had good armour too. I admire their bravery. They were responsible for repelling two huge invasions from the east, defeating the Persian Kings, Darius and Xerxes. Other Greek states helped in the wars but, in my not-to-be-relied-upon historical opinion, the Greek successes were mainly down to the Athenians.

Mostly I admire them for inventing democracy. It was a new idea that all citizens should have a say in the running of their nation. It was a brilliant innovation, and a step forward for the world. It's true that Athenian democracy did not extend to the universal franchise we'd expect today, but they made more progress in a generation than most other countries would manage in the next 2000 years.

Not everything about Athens was good. They spent a lot of time fighting and arguing with other Greek city-states. They made some disastrous foreign policy decisions, and the continual warfare led to their eventual downfall. Nonetheless, the great city-state of Athens, at its peak in the fifth century BC, left a huge mark on the world.

I've tried setting a novel in ancient Athens before, but it never really worked, and I abandoned these earlier efforts. It wasn't until I decided to make it revolve around Aristophanes that my book started to make sense. Aristophanes' riotous comedies helped to set the tone. If the Goddess of Buttercups and Daisies isn't exactly historical, containing as it does visits from nymphs and Amazons, well, Aristophanes laid the groundwork for this long ago, with his combination of real-life Athenians, Gods, and mythical creatures, all coming together in outlandish and improbable encounters. I'm very keen on Aristophanes. Despite the often-farcical nature of his plays, there is no-one better for telling you what life was actually like in the ancient city. These comedies might lack the grandeur of the great tragic writers, but they're the best place to learn about the sausage sellers, jurymen, farmers, and squabbling politicians who actually lived there.

Despite the various non-historical visitors who appear in the book, it is set in a real historical period in Athens. In 421 BC, Athens and Sparta had been at war for most of the past decade. Many Athenians were sick of the fighting, including Aristophanes. However there were plenty of people still in favour of war, which is where my book begins. Aristophanes did stage a play called *Peace* at the Dionysia in 421 BC, and there was a peace conference between Athens and Sparta. The comic poets Leucon and Eupolis both existed, and were Aristophanes' rivals for the prize, although little is known today of their work. Nicias and Hyperbolus were real politicians. Callias was the richest man in Athens, and Alcibiades was a notorious young aristocrat. Theodota the hetaera lived in Athens too. Her encounter with Socrates is described by Xenophon, and they do seem to get on rather well. As for Bremusa the Amazon and Idomeneus of Crete, they are both characters I borrowed from Greek Myth. Luxos's poem about the Goddess Athena unfortunately did not originate with me; it's my interpretation of an ancient Greek hymn to Athena.